# CIMARRON
# SEDUCTRESS

## By
## Lori Herter

Cover art by SelfPubBookCovers.com/Shardel

## Table of Contents

# CIMARRON SEDUCTRESS

## By Lori Herter

### *Chapter One*

Rafael de la Vega watched fondly as Annie awoke from a brief doze, her dusky long hair tousled, her body naked in his embrace. With a sensually satisfied sigh, she opened her drowsy eyes. She smiled at Rafael who was reclining beside her on the big bed, his arm lovingly resting beneath her breasts.

"Tired from your day teaching?" he asked, gently stroking her delicate skin. He always needed to remind himself that she was mortal, that he had to be careful not to injure her when in the throes of lovemaking. It was easy to forget, in the passion of the moment, that he had superhuman strength. Annie made him feel almost fully human again, and he liked to forget the fact that he was a vampire.

"The way you love me is so fulfilling." She ran her hand across his muscular chest. "You exhaust me, but I'm addicted. No one is like you."

Pleased with her answer, he slid his hand upward, covering her soft breast, teasing her nipple. She closed her eyes, an expression of serene pleasure on her face. "Yes, Rafael," she whispered. "I'm ready for more." Her hand found his swelling member and she smiled, urging him toward her.

Annie's uninhibited abandon delighted and further aroused him. He moved over her and began to penetrate her moist, warm femininity. Her eager gasps made him anticipate an even more exquisite climax than they'd already shared that evening.

But the moment was marred by the distant sound of a knock at the ranch house's front door.

Rafael lifted his head. "Francisco?" he muttered with irritation. "He knows this is our time together."

Francisco Santos, Rafael's horse trainer, usually came over to discuss business later in the evening. Rafael had requested him to do so after Annie had moved into the ranch house to live with Rafael a few months ago.

"Maybe there's an emergency with one of the horses?" Annie said. Rancho de la Noche had an international reputation in the equestrian world for the prize Appaloosas raised here. "You'd better answer," she reluctantly told him.

With a heavy sigh, Rafael rose from the bed and pulled on his jeans. They felt too tight over his erection as he zipped them up. He shrugged into his white shirt, not bothering to button it, and walked barefoot out of the bedroom. Hearing another, more energetic knock, he hurried through the living room into the small, blue-and-white-tiled entry hall. He swung open the big oak front door.

On his doorstep, under the light of a full moon, he was taken aback to see perhaps the most beautiful woman he'd ever met. A woman he hadn't laid eyes on for nearly half a century.

"Long time, no see, Rafael." Maisie Flowerday smiled eagerly at him, her dreamy blue eyes bright, her long, wavy, honey blonde hair flowing over her shoulders, highlighted by moon glow.

She wore tight denim jeans and cowboy boots. A low-cut, yellow knit top covered her ample breasts, and it was obvious she wore nothing underneath. Her nipples pressed against the thin material, the finishing touch to the easy, innocently wanton look that advertised her innately seductive nature. She'd possessed these attributes when she was only nineteen years of age, and still mortal.

Her highly-sexed beauty had undone Rafael decades ago. History was not going to repeat itself, he vowed, as he took a moment before replying. He needed to handle this correctly, give her no opportunity to cajole him. He might be wiser now, and he was deeply in love with Annie. Nevertheless, he was male, and he understood all too well that his gender suffered certain weaknesses.

"Why are you here?" He said the words in a sharp tone.

"To see you," Maisie cooed. She had a high, girlish voice that conveyed naivety. "You look handsome as ever."

"I have no interest in seeing you," he said, firmly.

She giggled. "Oh, don't be silly. You never could resist me."

"I'm immune to you, Maisie."

"I think you protest too much." Her eyes flirtatiously settled on his bared chest beneath his unbuttoned shirt.

As she reached to touch his ribs, Rafael backed away. His reaction didn't deter Maisie. Her gaze lowered to his zipper.

"Clearly you're happy to see me," she said, her voice growing a bit breathless. "You always did look *so* sexy when you're aroused. You can't hide it, you want me. Vampire sex is the best, as only you and I know. I've missed it *so* much! I was stupid to have left you. You must miss it, too."

Rafael closed his shirt in consternation, hoping the white shirttails would cover the bulge under his jeans. "I'm in love with a woman who is very precious to me. We were in bed when you knocked."

"You have a lover?" Maisie looked confused, like a little girl who didn't know what to do when the scoop of ice cream fell off her cone.

"Did you think I'd wait a half century hoping you might come back?" he said. "You ran off for greener pastures. I found someone new weeks after you left."

Maisie nodded. "That Indian girl. I thought you'd have gotten bored with her by now."

Rafael narrowed his eyes. How did she learn he'd had a relationship with Inez? "How do you know about her?"

"Oh, I snuck back a few times to check on you. Just curious. I was happy you weren't lonely. Really. So you turned the Indian girl? And she's still with you?"

"No, I didn't turn her and we separated years ago. Not that it's any of your concern."

"Oh." New hope dawned in Maisie's eyes. "Well, who are you with now? Is she as beautiful as me?" she asked blithely.

"She has an inner beauty you couldn't begin to understand. Or pretend to have. Who she is, is none of your business. I'm happy, happier than I've ever been. So go away. You're not welcome here." He took hold of the door, eager to shut it in her face.

But Maisie had an air of sadness now. "You're fortunate. I never did find those greener pastures, Rafael. I was only nineteen, and it seemed dull here on the ranch. After you turned me, I longed to explore my new vampire powers." She glanced at the door he was about to close and talked faster. "I met other men. Some really handsome hunks. I took their blood. It was fun having them under my control, to summon at my whim. But I never turned any of them." Her eyes met his. "Because none of them matched you. My mysterious Spanish conquistador." She gave him an adoring smile. "With your charming accent and awesome body. Oh, Rafael, I can't forget how fabulous sex with you was, after you made me a vampire, too. I'm lonely for you."

"Too bad. I'm not lonely," he replied, emphasizing the word *not*.

"Because your current lover has 'inner beauty?' My goodness. I had no idea you wanted a saint." Maisie's flawless face grew troubled. "Have you turned her?"

"No! I don't want her to become what you and I are," Rafael said with anger. "Now go."

He almost had the door shut on her. But possessing equal strength as he had, Maisie held the door half open.

"You don't have to tell her," she quickly argued. "You can keep your saintly mortal. Just slip off once

in a while to have a fabulous rough-and-tumble with
me."

"Go!" Rafael exclaimed.

# # #

Annie stood in the living room, out of view,
wide-eyed at the conversation she'd been
overhearing. She'd thrown on her blue robe, thinking
Francisco was at the door to inform Rafael about
some problem. But when she heard a female voice,
she'd quietly drawn closer to listen.

Upon hearing the suggestion that Rafael "slip
off" to have vampire sex, Annie decided she'd better
see who this brazen female was. She walked into the
entryway and stood beside and just behind Rafael.
When she gazed at the seductress he was talking to,
her heart began to sink. The woman was beautiful,
looked young and fresh, though Annie could tell from
her pointed incisors, similar to Rafael's, that she was
indeed a vampire. And apparently she'd once been
Rafael's lover. Though Annie felt reassured by
Rafael's declaration that he wanted no part of this
femme fatale's proposition, Annie nevertheless
wondered how any man could refuse what this
voluptuous female was offering.

Suddenly, the blue-eyed vampiress spotted Annie
as Rafael was angrily attempting to shut the door on
her.

"You must be the angel who has stolen Rafael's
heart," she said in a tone that was both accusing and
admiring.

Rafael turned, only now aware that Annie was
there. He let go of the door to wrap his arm around

Annie's shoulders. "I'm sorry about this. I'll get rid of her."

"I can see you're trying," Annie said archly, looking the other woman in the eye.

She smiled as she pushed the door back. "Hi, I'm Maisie. Maisie Flowerday. What's your name?"

"Annie Carmichael," Annie replied automatically, then wondered why this Maisie was being so friendly when her purpose was to have a rough-and-tumble with Rafael.

Annie couldn't help but be intimidated. Maisie looked as young as a teenager. Annie was thirty-five and beginning to notice faint crows-feet forming around her eyes. And while she had a trim figure, she couldn't begin to compete with Maisie's perky bosom and provocative curves.

"Annie, Rafael and I knew each other decades ago. I see he's with you now. That's nice. No reason we can't be friends."

Rafael looked up at the ceiling.

Bewildered, Annie stood her ground. "But I overheard you say you want to renew your old relationship with him. Why would we be friends?"

"Well," Maisie replied matter-of-factly, "we can share him."

"Are you out of your mind?" Rafael exclaimed. "I will not be untrue to Annie! She's my soul mate. I love her dearly."

Comforted by his words, Annie slipped her arms around Rafael, and he held her closer.

"There was a time when you wanted only me," Maisie sweetly reminded him. "We'd be at it all night, remember?"

"Just go," Rafael said in a low, harsh voice. "You're amoral and self-centered. A greedy hedonist! I want nothing to do with you."

"Oh, my. Calling me names." Maisie chuckled as she shook her head. "Like I said, you're protesting too much."

At that moment, Francisco walked up to the door, eyeing Maisie with curiosity in his brown eyes. He scratched the white hair above his ear a bit nervously.

"Sorry to interrupt," he said to Rafael. "I saw the big RV outside and wondered if a buyer had come by. Do you need me to show our horses?"

Annie looked past Maisie and Francisco to see that there was indeed a large white recreational vehicle parked in the driveway. Maisie's, apparently. It was certainly big enough to live in. And hold a coffin.

"Please come in, Francisco. We have business to discuss," Rafael instructed. "Maisie isn't here to buy a horse. She's leaving." He glared at her. "Now."

But Maisie kept her arm pressed against the door.

Francisco hesitated because she stood in his way. "Excuse me," he said. "Can't walk through you," he told her in an affable manner.

Surprisingly, Maisie let go of the door and stepped back, eyeing Francisco with interest. The white-haired horse trainer was in his mid-sixties, broad-shouldered and rather handsome with kind eyes and rugged hands. Annie wondered if Maisie was spontaneously drawn to any good-looking male.

Francisco walked through the door. When he was inside, Rafael unceremoniously shut it in Maisie's face. He locked the door's deadbolt. After giving

Annie a heartfelt embrace, he and Francisco headed to Rafael's office, adjacent to the living room.

Annie stood in front of the locked door, instinct making her fairly certain that Maisie was still on the other side.

Sure enough, Maisie's high voice came through. "You're still there, aren't you? Come over to the side window. We girls need to talk."

Annie drew in a long breath, eyeing the damask-draped window next to the front door. She knew she probably shouldn't, yet felt she needed to finish this confrontation. Steeling herself, she stepped up to the window, pushing aside the floor-length drapery. The doe-eyed beauty stood on the other side of the glass like a work of art created by some obsessed god of sensuality.

"Can you open the window?" Maisie asked, her voice muffled by the pane between them.

"No."

"Okay," Maisie said in an agreeable manner. "We can hear well enough. I want you to understand, Annie, that I bear you no ill will."

"What do you mean?"

"Only that I intend to get Rafael back. After all, I had him first. Before you were even born."

Annie stared at her, feeling a chill that didn't come from the cool of the night. "He loves *me*. He told you we're soul mates."

"Yeah, that's pretty sweet alright," Maisie said, a trace of wonder in her eyes. It quickly dissipated. "But, honey, you're no competition for me. Might as well face facts. Your frail mortal body can't give him the thrills I can."

Annie swallowed convulsively. "I heard him say you left him. Why do you want him back?"

Maisie nodded. "A fair question. I'll tell you. After he made me a vampire, I got restless. Wanted to be free. Wanted to try out other men, mortal men that I could control. I could hold Rafael with sex, but I couldn't control him. He wanted me to play house with him. That wasn't for me. So I left. And for decades, I had a blast, enjoying the feminine power only a female vampire can know."

Maisie lifted her shoulders in a helpless gesture. "But the last several years, I've gotten bored. I never forgot Rafael." Her eyes took on a what-was-I-to-do expression. "So I decided to come back. Be with him again, as his equal. See if I like being settled. And I do *so* miss the sex. Mortal men are pleasant, but they just don't have the stamina."

Annie sighed, feeling totally inadequate. She was well acquainted with Rafael's stamina.

"Sweetie, I can see what you're thinking and you're right," Maisie sympathized. "I can satisfy him way better than you can ever hope to. If you stay mortal. And Rafael said he won't turn you. So there we have the situation in a nutshell. I think the ideal solution is to share him. You can play house with him, and I'll give him the mind-blowing satisfaction I'm pretty sure he still craves."

"You don't love him," Annie said, growing angry. "You see him as a sex object."

"Oh, pooh." Maisie tossed her wavy hair back over her shoulder. "I love him. I never forgot him."

"You left him!"

"Well, I was a restless teen then. I've been stomping the planet for over 65 years now. I've finally come to appreciate what I lost when I left Rafael."

Her head beginning to ache, Annie rubbed her forehead. "If you really love him, why would you want to share him with me?"

Maisie looked at her with empathy. "I don't think the sharing would last long."

Annie stared at her. "You mean, he'd give up one of us?"

"You're a smart lady," Maisie said. "Which of us do you think he'd choose?"

Annie froze, feeling blood draining from her face.

Maisie smiled and in a breezy tone, said, "Bye for now." She turned and strolled to her RV, hips swaying, the long curls down her back bouncing with each lilting step.

Growing faint, Annie pulled the drapery back over the window, then numbly stumbled into the living room and collapsed on the leather couch.

In a few minutes, Rafael and Francisco walked out of the room that Rafael used as his office. Francisco said goodnight and left.

As Rafael walked up to the couch, Annie made the effort to pull herself together and sit up straight.

"Are you all right?" Rafael asked, sitting beside her, taking her wrist. "You're so cold," he said, rubbing her hand. "Not because of Maisie, I hope. She's nothing to me. She's gone."

Annie drew in a long breath and found her voice. "Not quite. She and I had a conversation through the window."

Rafael stared at her. "Why on earth—?"

"I needed to understand why she's here, what she's about."

"You shouldn't have," he said, disapproval in his eyes.

"Well, I did," Annie replied with impatience. "Maisie said you and I can play house, and she'll have you for the kind of sex she's sure you crave."

Rafael shut his eyes, seething with anger. "That's not going to happen! I promise you." He looked at Annie with steely resolution. "She never loved me. You do. For the first time I understand what it is to truly love someone. Why would I let her spoil what you and I cherish?"

"For vampire sex?"

"That's not what's important to me anymore," he assured her.

Annie stared at him with conviction. "I think you should turn me, Rafael. If you make me an immortal like you, I could give you what she can. How can I compete? I'm an ordinary thirty-five-year-old. She still looks like a promiscuous teenager."

"You're not ordinary!" Rafael took her by the shoulders and gave her a gentle shake. "There is no competition, Annie. You've already won. I'm yours, heart, mind and body. I love you."

Slowly nodding her head, Annie took in his words, positive that he sincerely meant them. "I believe you." She gazed at him steadily. "But men do tend to get taken in by a femme fatale like Maisie.

Maybe even a determined vampire who dearly loves a weak mortal."

"Never," Rafael insisted, his brows drawing together. "You are all I want."

"But I'm getting older. You're not. And neither is she. That's why you should turn me. Perform the blood ceremony you once described. I'm not afraid, Rafael. I'm willing."

Looking resolute, he shook his head. "I will not make you a creature of the night. It's I who must find a way to become mortal again. If only the Indian shaman hadn't died. He might have performed the secret ritual that could have made me whole. All I want and hope for is to live a normal human life with you."

Annie had heard him say this too many times to think she could find any argument that would change his mind.

"All right." She squeezed his hand, still holding hers. "So, would you tell me how you met Maisie? It might help if I knew the history. You encountered her before you met Inez?"

"Before Inez, yes." He stood and, keeping hold of her hand, urged her to come with him.

Annie followed. "Where are we going?"

"I'll begin by showing you something." Rafael led her into his office, then walked behind his desk, pushing aside his leather chair.

He began opening one desk drawer, then another, rifling through accumulated folders and papers, pamphlets on the care of horses that must have come from a veterinarian, and a loose stack of bright colored trophy ribbons.

"Your Appaloosas have placed first a lot," Annie commented, picking up the blue ones.

"They have," Rafael agreed with pride. He reached down to the bottom of a stack of folders. "It was probably too big to fit in a drawer," he muttered, dropping the folders and shoving the drawer closed.

Rafael paused, his brows knit together. "Where would it be?" Then his expression cleared. He peeked behind a metal file cabinet that stood against the wall. "I think this is it." He pulled out a glass-covered picture, about two feet long and one and a half feet wide, framed in wood. It had apparently been stashed away between the wall and the cabinet for many years, judging by the dust accumulated on the upper edge of the frame. He wiped off the dust with his hand and gave it to Annie.

She studied the image drawn on yellowing white paper with curious wonder. "It's a caricature of you." She grinned in amusement. "A good likeness, too." The black-and-white, pen-and-ink sketch captured his thick, unruly black hair, penetrating dark eyes, and even his subtle air of melancholy.

"Maisie drew it," he quietly told her. "Late in 1969, I think."

Annie looked up. "She's an artist?"

"Of sorts."

"But she's good," Annie had to admit. "She made this while you and she were together?"

"She drew it the night I met her," he explained, leaning against his oak desk. "I forget why I went into Cottonwood that evening. To buy something, or maybe I was bored at home here. Anyway, I discovered a carnival had been set up just outside of town, with merry-go-round rides for kids and booths where people were selling things. Maisie was there, sitting by a wooden easel, sketching people for a few dollars."

"She was still mortal?" Annie asked.

"Yes, and not even twenty years old. Though no innocent, despite her child-like voice and demeanor." He raked his hand through his hair. "I was several hundred years old, but hadn't learned much. Flirtatious, plucky young women were still my weakness."

"You mean, like the gypsy girl in Spain?"

He raised his eyebrows in a rueful way. "Who seduced me, expected me to marry her, and when I refused, her mother set the vampire curse on me— yes, like that gypsy girl. You'd think I would have learned. But no. Over the centuries I'd taken up with various women, some troublesome. All I had to do was take their blood and put them under my power. But Maisie got the better of me."

Annie felt he'd gotten ahead of himself in telling the story. She wanted details. "So you were at the carnival in town, and she was there making caricatures of people to earn money? You asked her to draw you?"

Rafael scratched his cheek. "Not exactly. I'd noticed her. She was stunningly beautiful, of course. She saw me looking at her and asked if I'd like her to do my caricature. I said no, at first. But then she said she thought I was so handsome, she'd do it for free. Being a thoughtless male, I was flattered. And being a creature who can't see himself in a mirror, it occurred to me that it might be interesting to get an idea of how

I looked after four hundred years. So I agreed, sat down in the folding chair by her easel, and she drew this." He pointed to the framed sketch in Annie's hands.

"I see. And then what?" Annie asked, already guessing the answer.

"After giving me the finished drawing, for which she didn't charge, she coyly offered herself to me. Also for free." He shrugged in a self-deprecating way. "Why would I refuse such an offer?"

"Well, at least she wasn't a prostitute," Annie quipped. "So you had sex, and then you took her blood to keep her under your control. Like with Inez."

He shook his head. "Not like Inez. I seduced Inez. Maisie seduced me. But, yes, until you, I would take a woman's blood to ensure that she would keep my secret."

"And so they'd be your sex slave for a while."

He bowed his head. "I wish you wouldn't put it that way."

Annie half-smiled. "I doubt they were unhappy." She paused, remembering something. "You once told me that there was a woman long ago that you turned, thinking she'd be your companion forever. But once you made her a vampire, she abandoned you. Was that Maisie?"

Rafael slowly nodded his head. "After I took her blood, she lived with me here. She didn't really have a home. She'd come from the east coast. I think her story was that she'd gone to Woodstock, the music festival. Met a guy from Arizona there. Her parents didn't like her new boyfriend, so she ran away with him. She got tired of him, but stayed in Arizona. Her parents were wealthy and kept sending her money to come home to New York, but she never did. She had a natural talent for drawing and started doing caricatures. To pass the time, and to meet men, I think."

"Why did you turn her?"

Rafael tilted his head in a regretful manner. "She begged me to. Said she thought being a vampire would be a big adventure. You see, she'd tried drugs, like LSD. I suppose she thought becoming a vampire would be a new kind of 'trip' to experience. And . . . she claimed she loved me. I was besotted with her. She argued that if she were immortal, too, she and I could be together forever."

Annie solemnly lowered her gaze, self-conscious that Maisie had used the same argument Annie gave him. This Maisie story was becoming increasingly unsettling. "So you performed the blood ceremony?"

He nodded.

"And then she left you?" Annie asked in a puzzled tone. "Why?"

"She walked out after only a couple of weeks," Rafael said. "The more she got used to her vampire strength, the more she wanted to go off and test her powers. Without me trying to caution her. She accused me of keeping her hemmed in, like her parents had." He shrugged. "She was a new vampire. I thought she needed the benefit of my centuries of knowledge. Maybe I *was* being protective. Stupid of me to think a female like her needed protection."

"And so she just left? Did she say goodbye?" Annie prompted, needing to know every last tidbit.

"She said I'd become her policeman, keeping tabs on her. She'd had enough—wanted to be free. Packed up her easel and all her clothes and left one night. I was crushed. Felt completely taken in by her. I'd been so enchanted with her ultra-feminine charm, it took me a while to understand that she was simply a headstrong adolescent. Seeing her tonight, I don't think she's changed. She probably has no plan or purpose, except to lure me back. Her wanderlust has gotten old. So she thinks bedding a vampire will give her a renewed high. She's immature, still that hippie who expects to have fun all the time."

"She's certainly a narcissist," Annie agreed.

"I learned my lesson," Rafael continued. "Soon I found Inez, a much more grounded person, who never asked me to turn her. I wouldn't have anyway. I'd learned that lesson, too."

"Is that why you won't turn me?" Annie asked with a sad little smile. "You think there's that small chance that I might get carried away with vampire power and run off?"

Rafael seemed at a loss how to reply. After a moment, he said, "Do you really want to spend your days in a coffin? How would you continue your career teaching archeology at the university? Do you want to crave blood and have to rob blood banks?"

Annie swallowed hard. She had to admit, she did feel some revulsion in the pit of her stomach at his description. "No," she replied. "But if it's the only way you and I can be together . . . ." She paused as a new question came to her. "After you turned Maisie, did you build her a coffin?"

He hesitated. "I was going to. She left before I could."

"Where did she rest? Did you take her to the kiva, where I discovered you?"

"No, she had no interest in the Anasazi ruin."

"Where did she rest in the day, then?"

Rafael's expression grew even more hesitant, and Annie intuited that the answer was something he'd rather not have to tell her.

Finally, he met her gaze. "She shared my coffin."

Annie's shoulders drooped. She set the framed drawing on the desk. "That seems almost more intimate than the all-night romps you two had. You shared your coffin to protect her from the sun. When dusk came, you awoke with her. That luscious body on top of yours. That's something you can't do with me."

"Annie . . . ." He reached to take her in his arms.

She backed away. "I can't talk about this anymore. I need some time alone."

### # # #

Inez stepped out onto her small porch to enjoy the brisk evening air. It was mid-March, and nights were still chilly on the chaparral. The duplex in which she lived was located a short walk from Rafael's Spanish-tiled stucco home and built in the same style. Francisco lived next to her in the duplex's other apartment. She thought she'd heard him go out earlier than usual. He generally met with Rafael later in the evening to discuss business.

Looking toward the ranch's driveway, which ended in front of Rafael's house, the sight of a large, white RV startled her. Who would be visiting? Rafael didn't have many acquaintances. A customer who was in a hurry to buy an Appaloosa?

And then she saw Francisco leaving Rafael's house. As he walked onto the driveway, the door of the RV opened. A young woman, gorgeous as a movie star, stepped down from the vehicle and moseyed up to Francisco, who stopped to talk to her. Who on earth was she?

Inez had protected her heart from the gentle advances Francisco had been making toward her. At sixty-five, she'd convinced herself that she was past the age to be wooed. But seeing Francisco become animated as he chatted with this nubile stranger who coquettishly tossed her locks of wavy hair as she talked, Inez realized she felt a bit jealous. Maybe she cared for Francisco more than she wanted to admit.

Wise enough to know that envy was unseemly in a mature woman—and useless—Inez nevertheless stepped off the porch and quietly walked up to the parked RV.

As she approached, Francisco turned and saw her. "Hey, Inez."

"Hello, Francisco. What's going on?" Inez stood beside him and turned her eyes to the young woman.

"This is Maisie," Francisco said. "A . . . um, an acquaintance of Rafael's."

Maisie returned Inez's questioning gaze. "Nice to meet you," she said with a smile.

Inez immediately noticed Maisie's teeth. Her incisors were a bit too long. Not so much that the average person would particularly notice. But to the experienced eye, they were a clue as to the dark nature of the creature who possessed them.

Inez knew very well what vampire teeth looked like. She'd been Rafael's secret lover for thirty years. How often in those years had she willingly let him drink from her, feeling pleasure at giving him her own blood for his sustenance. She used to wear a bandana around her neck to cover the marks his teeth had made. The small wounds were healed now, though subtle scars remained.

Francisco, however, seemed unaware of all this. Though he'd worked for Rafael for forty-five years or so, Francisco apparently had no suspicion his boss was one of the undead. Rafael had the power to make men forget what they should not have seen. Nor did Francisco seem to suspect that for decades Inez had had trysts with Rafael in the wee hours of the night, until he finally let her go about fifteen years ago. There were more reasons than her mature age that kept Inez from encouraging Francisco's romantic overtures.

Maisie turned her blue-eyed gaze back to Francisco. "So, you were telling me about Annie."

"Um . . . well, she's been with Rafael for a few months now." Francisco seemed unsure what to say.

"How did they meet?"

Francisco shrugged. "I don't know. Never asked."

"Really?" Maisie said, raising her eyebrows. "Like she just appeared one day, out of thin air?"

Inez wondered why Maisie was so curious about Annie.

"Well, Annie was engaged to the man who owns the ranch next to this one," Francisco said. "The announcement was in the paper. But she left him at the altar . . . ," he paused as Inez tugged on his arm, ". . . and now she's with Rafael." He glanced at Inez, who gave him a speaking look. "That's all I know," he hurried to add, looking back at Maisie. "I don't pry into his personal life."

Inez quietly took a breath, wishing Francisco hadn't said as much as he had. Though when he told Maisie that it was all he knew, he was probably telling the truth. Inez continued to cling to his arm in a friendly way, something she didn't ordinarily do.

Maisie's glance seemed to take this in, no doubt intuiting that Inez wouldn't let him say any more. She smiled at them. "You two make a cute couple."

Inez's head went back, but Francisco looked quite pleased with her observation.

"I'll be off now," Maisie blithely told them. "Say, is there a fun place in Cottonwood? Like a bar or a diner the locals favor?"

*A diner?* Inez wondered what Maisie was angling for. Vampires don't eat.

"The Turquoise Toad Bar and Grill is a favorite place," Francisco told her. "They have good food and a well-stocked bar. Dart board and foosball, too." He gave her directions to find it.

"I'll check it out. Thank you, Francisco." Maisie gave him a sugary smile.

Inez nodded to her, happy to see her turn away from them and step up into her RV.

Tugging on Francisco's arm again, lightly this time, she encouraged him to start walking toward the duplex. "She's so sweet you could spread her on bread," Inez commented under her breath.

"Sure is," he replied, looking a little puzzled. "Awfully pretty, too. I wonder what connection she has with Rafael? I got the impression he wasn't pleased to see her. Annie looked kind of grim, too."

"Annie saw her? That's not good. I suspect Maisie may be a former girlfriend of Rafael's," Inez said. "I don't trust her. I think she's up to something."

During her years with Rafael, he'd told her about some of his previous women. She remembered there was one in particular that he said he'd turned, but then she ran off.

"Come to think of it," Francisco said, "Maisie looks a lot like a beautiful girl who was with him for a while. Don't remember her name. She was an artist and drew a quick sketch of me one evening. I envied Rafael, I have to admit. But pretty soon, I didn't see her around anymore. Rafael never said what happened, and I didn't think it was my place to ask. All that was a long, long time ago, though. I was young then, maybe twenty, twenty-one. That girl would be about the same age as us now."

"You mean, old?" Inez quipped, while thinking that Maisie might indeed be the mistress who was Inez's predecessor. The girl Rafael made a vampire.

Francisco reached behind Inez and gave her long grey braid a playful yank. "Who are you calling old! We're in our prime."

Inez laughed. Francisco, she'd discovered since she'd moved to Rancho de la Noche a few months ago, was one of the few people who could make her laugh. She'd become a very serious person, weighed down by her past. Francisco was the opposite. He knew how to savor every moment, how to enjoy life minute by minute. Wouldn't it be nice if she could learn how to live that way, too?

"How about some tea?" he asked. "I'll make it."

She hesitated. "You mean, in your kitchen?"

"You always seem reluctant to enter my place," he said in a kind way. "I'm a nice guy. The horses all trust me."

"I know. I . . . I'm just not used to . . ." Inez sighed, not sure how to finish her sentence.

"I'm not asking you for a date," he said, apparently guessing what made her hesitate. "It's just tea. I might have a few cookies in my cupboard, if you don't think that's overdoing it."

Inez found herself laughing again. "All right. Thank you, Francisco."

# # #

Annie sat alone in the dining room at the big oak table, strewn with papers and archeology journals. The old rustic table had begun to serve as her desk, now that she was living with Rafael. She still kept her condo in Tucson for convenience, since it was near the University of Arizona where she taught archeology. But she'd come to consider Rafael's ranch house her true home.

Recovering from her conversation with Maisie and learning that decades ago the voluptuous vampiress had shared Rafael's coffin, Annie told herself she needed to be strong. She believed with all her heart that Rafael loved her, and only her. But Maisie's sudden intrusion was disconcerting.

She rubbed her eyes, thinking she needed to get more sleep. She often looked tired. That was the downside of living with a vampire. The only time she could be with him was after dark. She loved their lovemaking, but often it came at the expense of a full night's sleep. Not that she was willing to give up her hours in Rafael's arms. Especially not now, when his former playmate intended to lure him back. Annie had to learn to function on four or five hours of sleep on days she had classes and needed to leave early to drive to Tucson.

She heard footsteps and looked up to see Rafael come into the dining room. He paused just inside the open doorway.

Studying her, he asked, "Are you all right? Had enough time alone?"

Annie nodded. "I'll be okay."

He slowly stepped up to her chair, then kneeled beside her. "I adore you, you know. I worship you."

Annie smiled and stroked his face. "I adore you, too. And I appreciate the way you so freely express your love. To me, and in front of others. But this Maisie seems like a force to be reckoned with. Your declaration of devotion to me didn't faze her one bit."

"Don't worry," he said in a doting tone, taking her hands in his. He chuckled. "If she causes any trouble between us, I'll drive a stake through her heart."

Annie drew back, unsettled by his words, though he seemed to be joking. "You mean . . . is the folklore about that really true? The way to destroy a vampire is to hammer a stake into them?"

"It's more than folklore," he assured her. "The only ways to finish off a vampire forever are to put a wooden stake through their heart, or keep them from their coffin when daylight comes."

"But, you wouldn't really do that to her, would you?" Annie asked. "It's like murdering her."

"She's already dead," he pointed out.

"You know what I mean," she argued. "I don't like her, or the fact that she exists, but—"

Rafael leaned upward to kiss her. "You are such an honorable woman. Something Maisie could never be. I cherish you. I value you most highly. I'll never feel that way about her."

"Thank you," Annie whispered, tears in her eyes.

"And I don't think there will ever be a need to destroy her. When she finds she'll get nowhere with me, she'll move on to someone else. She's flighty and easily distracted. Needs to be entertained. Remember, she got bored with me."

Annie placed her hands on his broad shoulders. "But what about the vampire sex she wants? How can that not be a temptation?"

"When I'm with you, I feel like your very soul fuses with mine. It gives me hope that I may still have a soul. I've never felt that way before. For me, you are the only woman in the world."

Tears streamed down Annie's cheeks. "You're the only one for me, too." She leaned forward as he wrapped his arms around her.

He kissed her soundly. Soon his hands pushed down her robe from her shoulders, and he kissed and caressed her breasts. As he teased her hardening nipples, he murmured, "We never got to finish making love."

Her breaths coming fast with anticipation, she said, "No, we didn't." She smiled. "I think we should."

He stood, picked her up in his arms, and carried her to the bedroom.

# # #

Inez sat at Francisco's small kitchen table covered with red and white, plaid-patterned oilcloth. He filled the mug he'd placed in front of her with tea from an old Brown Betty teapot. He filled his own cup, then set the teapot on the table.

"My wife always used this pot," he explained. "She didn't like putting a tea bag in a cup."

"You still miss her?" Inez asked with empathy.

"She passed away about five years ago now. I'll always remember our years together, but life goes on. Just wish my grandchildren could have known her. They're all too little."

"That's a shame," Inez agreed. "Was she Mexican heritage, like you?"

"Yes. We met in high school in Phoenix. You said you're from the Laguna Pueblo in New Mexico?"

"My mother was Indian and my father was Mexican. He was doing some work at the Pueblo when he met my mother. I have an older brother who still lives there. Not in good health, though."

Francisco studied her with cautious curiosity. "So why did you never marry?"

Inez drew in a long breath and gazed down at the steaming cup in front of her. "That's a hard question to answer," she carefully replied. "Then again, maybe the answer is simple. No one ever asked me."

"You must have kept yourself hidden away at Logan's ranch. Until I started going to church again, after my wife died, I never saw you around anywhere."

That wasn't quite true, Inez knew, but didn't correct him. When she'd first become Rafael's mistress and was under his power, he'd mentally summon her in the night. She would borrow one of Brent Logan's horses and ride over to Rafael's home. One night, after her hours with Rafael, she walked out of the ranch house at sunrise, only to discover that the horse she'd borrowed had gotten loose and run off. Rafael had retired to his coffin by then, so she'd had to ask a very young Francisco to drive her back to the Logan Ranch, where she worked and lived. She was so obviously embarrassed, he must have guessed she'd spent the night with his boss. But he remained polite and asked no questions as he drove her home.

Today, if Francisco recalled that incident at all, he seemed to have no suspicion that the grey-haired woman in the broomstick skirt and blouse sitting at his table was the same person he brought back to the Logan spread that morning. What would he think of her, if he ever made that connection?

"Brent kept me busy," she said. "I'd drive into town to buy food. Part of my job as their cook. But you probably seldom went grocery shopping."

"My wife took care of that," Francisco said. "And then my daughter, who lived where you do now. After my daughter and her husband moved out—he got a good job offer, I think I told you—I had to fend for myself. Survived on cereal and sandwiches until Rafael hired you to be our cook. The ranch hands say they've never had it so good."

Inez smiled. "I'm happy to hear it."

"Say, I forgot the cookies." Francisco rose from the table. He opened a cabinet above his refrigerator and pulled out a cellophane wrapped package of Oreos. "I should put some on a plate," he said, opening another cabinet.

"No, don't bother," Inez told him. "I'll have one right from the box."

He set it on the table. She figured out how to open it, and took a cookie. He sat across from her again and munched on a cookie, too. They were silent for a moment.

"Pearl Girl is getting big," Inez said, referring to the Appaloosa colt Rafael had given her on the evening he'd hired her as cook and invited her to live in the duplex. Brent Logan had fired her that morning. "She's so sweet. She recognizes me and comes over for her carrots."

"I've noticed," Francisco said. "She likes me, but you're her favorite. I can tell. Rafael gave you quite a gift in Pearl Girl. She could turn out to be a prize-winner."

Inez nodded, pausing to consider if she should try to find out how much Francisco really knew about Rafael.

"Rafael was very generous to me," Inez began. He'd given Inez the colt to try to make up for the years he'd stolen from her. The reason she'd never married was because Rafael kept her under his power all through her child-bearing decades. Even if she'd had the opportunity to meet a potential husband, Rafael had controlled her mind and heart. "You've worked for him for many years," she said to

Francisco. "Do you consider him a friend, as well as your boss?"

"I think so," Francisco replied, nodding with hesitation. "We rarely disagree. I think he trusts me and relies on me." He scratched his nose. "But he's not the kind of friend I'd go to the Turquoise Toad and have a beer with on a Saturday night."

Inez softly bit her lip, worried about asking her next question. But she went ahead. "Rafael looks so young, doesn't he?" She took on an amiable, admiring tone. "Fit and strong. Though you're still very fit, too."

"Thanks," Francisco replied, looking happy with her compliment. "You're right, he does appear young, and he must be at least my age." He shrugged. "Maybe he dyes his hair black," he said with a chuckle. "Though he doesn't seem like the type to be concerned about that."

"And he has so few wrinkles," Inez commented.

Francisco paused, apparently trying to recall. "Women notice stuff like that more than we men. He's my boss, so we talk about horses and business. I guess I don't pay much attention to how he looks."

Inez smiled to herself. Perhaps Francisco had something there. Men didn't tend to notice details—unless, of course, a good-looking woman was passing by. Which reminded her of Maisie. Francisco did seem to be distracted by *her* looks.

"That Maisie Flowerday was sure young and beautiful," Inez said in an airy, abstract way.

"Oh, yeah," Francisco agreed. "Very easy on the eyes. But Rafael didn't like her, so I hope she doesn't come back. Seemed to be some history there that I'd just as soon not know." He glanced at Inez and placed his elbow on the table, his chin in his hand. "Now what made you say that about her?"

Inez blinked. "Well, just making conversation."

"Don't you be jealous because I got a little befuddled around her. No matter how old a guy gets, he always finds himself turning to putty when confronted with a pretty girl."

"I'm not jealous," she objected.

"Aw, I hoped maybe you were," he said, his manner only half-joking. "You know, now that you and I drive to mass on Sunday mornings together, people think we're a pair. Even that Maisie girl said we were a cute couple."

Inez wet her lips. "Can't help what people think and say. We go to mass together because it's convenient. Why would we drive separately?"

"Inez, Inez. Always so practical." He raised his eyebrows. "I liked it when you took my arm, when I was talking to Maisie."

"I was trying to keep you from saying too much. She's a stranger. How Rafael met Annie is none of her business."

"I know," Francisco agreed. "You were right to curb my blathering. But, still, I liked it when you took my arm. You can do that anytime. It won't even look odd, since people see us as a pair already."

Inez gazed down at her half-full cup. "I'll . . . keep that in mind." She looked up. "It's time I leave. Thank you for the tea and cookies." She rose from the table.

"Anytime, Inez," Francisco said as he walked with her through his living room to his front door.

"And you don't have to come and go through this door. There's the doorway between your living room and mine. You keep your side locked, I know. But feel free to open it and knock on mine anytime."

"Okay," she said, beginning to feel a bit lightheaded as she walked outside. She wasn't used to being pursued. "I'll keep that in mind, too."

He grinned in a knowing way. She could tell by his bemused eyes that he understood she wouldn't be knocking on his door anytime soon.

"Goodnight, Inez. See you tomorrow. The corral after lunch? Check on Pearl Girl?"

"Yes. 'Night," she replied, happy to step off his porch and walk the few steps to her own. He waited on his porch until she walked through her door. Relieved, she closed it and locked it. She sat on her upholstered easy chair and looked down at the braided oval rug on the hardwood living room floor.

Most single women her age would probably be pleased, even thrilled, to have a nice-looking man so interested in them. But the weight of her strange, some might say sordid, past never left Inez's shoulders. Would Francisco be so eager to be paired with her, if he knew her history? He didn't even know Rafael was a vampire. Was her secret former life with Rafael something that could forever remain secret? Should she tell Francisco she used to be Rafael's mistress? It would be the most honest thing to do. But that would mean revealing Rafael's true nature.

It was such an unsavory puzzle, Inez thought, rubbing her eyes. And no solution seemed at hand.

*Chapter Two*

Maisie walked into the Turquoise Toad and paused inside the open glass door for a few moments as she checked out the place. It wasn't large. The polished mahogany bar stood along the wall to the left. She was happy to see there were no mirrors hung behind it. Just shelves with an array of liquor bottles and glasses of various sizes and shapes. Small tables occupied the center portion of the hardwood floor and booths lined the windowed wall to the right. At the back a foosball table and dartboard were available for patrons to use.

She wouldn't be ordering any food, of course, so she ambled up to the bar and took a leather padded stool. Several men sat at the far end of the bar. Since she had come there looking for information and not to find a boy toy for the evening, she stayed on her own. The bartender, a tall, middle-aged chap with balding brown hair came up to her.

"What'll you have?"

"A small glass of port," Maisie replied.

She'd found her vampire system could tolerate port or sherry, but only a bit. Too much made her a little ditsy, and she never wanted to risk blabbing anything that would reveal her secret nature. In her own mind, she called herself an *Immortal*. *Vampire* sounded rude, even scary. Though *Vampiress* had a certain panache. And *Undead*—well, that just didn't have a classy ring to it at all. But she couldn't risk inadvertently referring to herself using any of these terms. At least, not until she'd taken someone's blood and put them under her power.

Not tonight, though.

While she waited for the bartender to return, she saw an object on a small wooden pedestal placed on the back counter, beneath the shelves of bottles. It looked like a colorful stone.

"What's that?" she asked, pointing, when the bartender set the glass of amber liquid in front of her.

He turned to see what she was asking about. "Oh, you mean our namesake? That's the Turquoise Toad." He picked it up and showed it to her. "Carved by a Zuni craftsman years ago."

She grinned, studying the smoothly polished stone as he held it on the palm of his hand. "It does look like a toad. That's real turquoise?"

"Sure is. A quality chunk of it, too." He set it back on display, then faced her again. "I'm Kevin, by the way. You new in Cottonwood?" He looked like he was trying not to focus on her cleavage.

"Sort of. I'm Maisie. Looks like you do a nice business here."

"Sure do," he said matter-of-factly.

"You must know most of the people in these parts then," she said.

"Probably."

Affecting an effortless innocence, she began her probe. "I heard someone talking about a local rancher who was supposed to marry a woman named Annie, but he was jilted on his wedding day. What an awful thing. Made me feel so bad for the poor fellow."

Kevin half-smiled and nodded. "Yup. That's been gossip fodder for months now. I was one of the hundred or so guests invited to the wedding. Ranch house was all decorated with flowers for the ceremony. The judge was there to marry them. And then Brent got up and announced that his bride had left him in the lurch. Packed up, moved out, with only a note to say she'd decided she couldn't go through with the wedding."

"How dreadful for him. His name is Brent?"

"Brent Logan. His spread is a dozen miles up the highway."

A memory from the past came to Maisie. "The Logan Ranch. It's next to Rancho de la Noche?"

Kevin's eyebrows rose. "So you're familiar with the area."

"Oh, from a long time ago," she said, casually. "This Brent, is he the grandson of Joe Logan?"

The bartender nodded. "Right. You're so young, how would you know about old Joe? He died when I was a kid."

Maisie pursed her lips, knowing a kissable mouth tended to distract men, while she thought of an answer. She'd gotten careless revealing she knew who Joe Logan was. "Um, I suppose my grandfather must have talked about him before he died."

"I see. Who was your grandfather?" Kevin asked with interest.

Oh, darn, she'd talked herself into a corner. "Well, Grandpa Flowerday was from New York, but he met Joe Logan somehow and came out to visit him at the Logan spread," she improvised. "He used to love to talk about his time on a real cowboy ranch."

Kevin smiled and started wiping the bar with a cloth, apparently buying her fiction. "Is that your name, too? Flowerday?"

"It's a pretty name, isn't it? I'm lucky to inherit it."

"A pretty name for a very pretty girl," Kevin said.

"Thank you. So you must know Brent Logan if you were invited to his wedding. Does he come here much?"

"Oh, yeah, about once a week. He comes in with his foreman and they have dinner together. Brent likes to talk over their cattle business away from the other ranch employees."

"On a weekend, I suppose," she said, fishing.

"No, usually mid-week." Kevin grinned. "Why? You hoping to meet him since he's still single?"

Maisie tossed her hair and gave him an arch, coy look. "Do I look like a gold-digger?"

He laughed. "You look like a million bucks to me. Brent would be a good catch, all right." He rubbed his thumb against his fingertips, indicating wealth. "He probably could use someone like you to cheer him up."

"Well, then, I'll have to come here often," she said in her soft, high voice. She gave him a wide-eyed blink. "When he does come in, would you point him out to me?"

Kevin laughed again. "You got a deal, Miss Maisie. Hang out here as much as you like. I've a feeling you'll be good for business."

"Thank you!"

As he turned away to check on his other customers at the far end of the bar, Maisie relaxed and sipped her port. That went well, she decided with satisfaction. It should be only a matter of days before she met Brent Logan. Contrary to what she allowed the bartender to think, she wasn't out to get Brent for herself. Her purpose was to influence him to try to win Annie back. If Brent attempted, with Maisie's advice and encouragement, to reclaim his fiancée, it would create a wedge between Annie and Rafael. Once they split, Maisie would be right there to pick up the pieces. Coaxing a heartbroken Rafael into a phenomenal, nightlong romp with her was all it would take. He'd forget all about his darling Annie, no problem.

Maisie smiled as she made the tawny liquid in her glass swirl. This was going to be fun!

# # #

The next morning, Annie drove to the University of Arizona campus and parked near the red brick building where she taught. Dressed in a long brown skirt, boots and a white blouse, she entered the stately building. She should have been thinking about the Pueblo Archeology class she'd be teaching an hour from now. Instead, Maisie Flowerday kept intruding into her thoughts. She had a feeling Maisie would find some way to put herself in Rafael's path again, and soon. While Annie trusted Rafael's intention to be true, being realistic, what male, vampire or mortal, could resist Maisie?

On autopilot, Annie soon found herself walking down the hallway where most of the archeology professors' offices were located. Getting out her key from her shoulder bag as she approached her door, from the corner of her eye she saw a tall, slim man walking down the hall toward her. Oh, no . . . Frank Florescu.

Annie pulled her wits together and hurried to unlock her door. She ignored him and hoped he'd walk by her. He hadn't said much to her since she'd been promoted instead of him to full professor. *Keep going, keep walking*, she mentally willed him.

She flinched as he stopped and leaned against her door jamb. His sudden nearness unsettled her. She stepped sideways while he seemed to be trying to appear nonchalant.

"Dr. Carmichael," he greeted her in a cold, polite manner.

"Dr. Florescu." She mimicked his tone, but avoided looking at him, fiddling with her door key instead.

"Need help with that?" he asked.

"The lock sticks sometimes," she said. "I'll get it open, thanks."

He didn't move, making her more nervous.

Finally, he straightened up, pushed strands of thinning brown hair off his forehead and said, "You may think you've outsmarted me. You may have succeeded in pulling the wool over our colleagues' eyes and the powers-that-be around here. But I know the truth. You're the consort of a vile creature. I don't care how handsome and charming de la Vega appeared to everyone when you brought him to the holiday party. He's one of the undead."

"Don't be ridiculous."

"My Romanian grandfather told me what righteous people in Eastern Europe did to rid themselves of such abhorrent beings. A stake through the heart—"

"Stop it!" she hissed at him. "You're deluded. Listen to yourself. It's no wonder they chose me instead of you for the promotion. Everyone thinks you've gone off the rails with your vampire talk. No one believed your claims about me—they're all laughing at you. You've only succeeded in damaging your own career, not mine."

"Because they don't understand that supernatural evil exists," he replied, incensed. "I know better. A woman like you shouldn't even be a member of the faculty. You're a vampire's whore."

"How dare you call me that!" she shot back, trembling with anger.

"What should a woman be called who willingly gives her body to an unholy being to appease his unnatural lust?"

"He's not a vampire!" she exclaimed with fury. She loved Rafael so, it wasn't difficult to deny the truth.

"I saw his fangs," Florescu said. "The kid at the party taking pictures noticed he didn't show up in the camera's digital photos. When de la Vega realized I'd discerned his secret, he left."

"None of that proves he's a vampire," Annie argued.

Contempt filled the professor's hazel eyes. "Either you're too stupid to see the obvious, or he's got you mesmerized." He pushed aside the collar of her blouse before she could back away. "Your carotid is still untouched. Why do you let him defile you? I know how to rescue you from his clutches—"

She struck his probing hand with her key, making him wince. "Get away from me. You're the one who's vile!"

Florescu's thin, angular face grew red and his eyes darkened with revenge. "You'll be sorry." He glared at her, then stepped away.

As he continued down the hallway, she managed to unlock her door with shaking fingers. Once inside, she locked it again and sat down on the nearest chair, the one in front of her desk that students used when they came to discuss their term papers. She buried her head in her hands, recovering. No one had ever called her a whore. No one had ever threatened her. What did he mean, *You'll be sorry*?

Florescu might indeed know Rafael's secret. But the professor seemed to be growing more and more crazed. What should she do?

Annie took some deep, slow breaths to calm herself. She had a class to teach. A quarter of an hour later, she felt more together. Gathering her class notes, she headed to her lecture hall.

The class went smoothly and her students didn't seem to detect that she'd been shaken to the core. Feeling exhausted, she walked back to her office, filed her notes in her metal cabinet, then, seeing Florescu nowhere about, she headed to the faculty lounge.

As she was inserting a K-cup into the coffee machine, two of her colleagues, Joan Wilcox and Tom Harvey came in. Both were professors of Archeology.

"Annie," Joan greeted her with a sunny smile in her blue eyes. In her mid-forties, the mother of college age children, she still looked youthful with her blonde hair and slim figure. She wore khaki pants and a sweater.

"Hey there," Tom said. Almost forty, also married with children, he had red hair and freckles. "How's it going?"

Annie took her filled cup from the machine. "Fine, except for Frank Florescu." She took a chair at one of the small, square tables in the lounge.

"Oh, no," Joan said, sitting down across from her at the table. "What happened?"

As Tom got coffee for Joan and himself, Annie described her encounter with Florescu, recalling as much of the conversation as she could. "He finished by threatening me with, 'You'll be sorry.'"

"Geez," Tom said, setting down a cup in front of Joan. He took a seat at the table with them. "He's been looking belligerent and keeping to himself ever since you won the Outstanding Contribution to the Field of Archeology Award and got your promotion. But I never imagined he had that much venom in him."

"He's lost everyone's respect with all his crazy vampire talk," Joan said, shaking her head. "Like a lot of blowhards, he's probably just full of hot air. He'll get over it."

Annie took in a deep breath and let it out in a long exhale. "He doesn't seem to be getting over it. His vampire ideas are festering in his mind. He's getting a little scary."

She saw Tom and Joan eye each other with concern. Neither one apparently could come up with an argument that might reassure her. As the three of them sat drinking coffee, the silence at the table made Annie grow cold, despite the hot cup in her hands. She feared what steps Florescu might take that could prove Rafael's immortal nature.

How could she protect the dearest love of her life? Rafael had superhuman strength and could easily subdue any mortal man who tried to physically attack him. But could Florescu succeed in revealing Rafael's secret? What if the professor managed to make people believe that vampires existed? She had to allow that Florescu had truth on his side.

Should she tell Rafael? That was a conundrum. If Rafael knew, he might be able to take some steps to protect himself. But on the other hand, he might worry about her and her career. Annie felt she could take care of herself and didn't want Rafael to be concerned. Surely there was some way to keep Florescu from causing problems. Joan, Tom, and other colleagues at the university already thought he was no longer mentally sound. Perhaps it was Frank Florescu who should be worried about his future.

## Chapter Three

That evening, Maisie came back to the Turquoise Toad, carrying her drawing pad and pen. For now she'd left her easel at home, "home" being her RV, newly purchased about a year ago. She'd been investing her inheritance from her wealthy parents, getting hot tips from a savvy broker she'd seduced. Money was not an issue for her. She had more than she needed for her easy, vagabond existence.

She drew caricatures for fun and to meet men, not for the token dollars she received for her pen and ink portraits. It suited her purpose if the men she met thought she was only eking out a living. It made them feel protective toward her, so they never guessed that they were the ones who might not be safe. Not that she ever meant anyone, even her conquests, any harm. Those whose blood she took never seemed unhappy to find themselves bonded to her, living at her beck and call. In fact, she kept them quite happy.

Until she eventually left them. That was always a little sad. Once she mentally shut down the bond she had with a man, he was perfectly free again. Maybe he never got over her, but she couldn't help that, could she?

It bothered her, miffed her in fact, that Rafael had apparently forgotten her. Claimed to be in love with his saintly Little Orphan Annie. But she'd soon remedy that. *Whatever Maisie wants, Maisie gets*, she reminded herself as she strolled up to the bar.

Kevin came up to greet her as she set her drawing pad on the polished wood.

"Hey, Maisie. What's this?"

"I'm a caricature artist," she said, standing proudly in her high-heeled, tall black boots. "Wondered if maybe you'd let me set up my easel here. It might be good business for both of us."

She watched the bartender's eyes taking in her wavy hair, and her curves on display in her short, tight, black leather skirt and ruffled white blouse with its plunging neckline.

"You know how to draw?" Kevin said with a doubtful smile.

"How about if I do a caricature of you?" she offered. "You can judge for yourself."

He nodded. "Have at it. You want me to stand here?"

"Sure. Strike a pose." She took a seat on a bar stool, set the bottom of the drawing pad on her lap and let it lean against the edge of the bar. She began to sketch, using a special black poster marker she'd discovered a few years ago in an art supply store. She used a thin sliver of wax-based crayon for shading.

In about ten minutes she was finished and turned the drawing pad around for Kevin to see. The caricature showed him with a big, toothy smile, pouring foamy beer into a glass with the carved toad sitting on the bar, as if watching.

"Next time, I'll bring a turquoise colored pencil to fill in the toad," Maisie said.

Kevin studied it with a smile that became an appreciative chuckle. "Very nice. It even looks like me. And you added the toad, too. I think I'll frame this and hang it up here."

Maisie grinned. "Glad you like it. So, can I set up my easel?"

"Go ahead," he replied, looking pleased.

Her plan was going well so far. She wanted to look like she came to the Turquoise Toad to make money doing caricatures, and not like a bar floozy who hung out there every night. If she was going to impress Brent Logan, she needed to keep up appearances. Look alluring, yet respectable. Fortunately, long ago she'd discovered her ability to draw allowed her to keep that balance. Men instantly adored her.

She didn't do many pictures of women.

For the next few evenings, Maisie arrived at the Turquoise Toad shortly after sunset. Her RV was parked down the street by an empty lot. She rose from her coffin in the part of the vehicle meant to be a bedroom, decided which outfit to wear, and combed her hair by feel, since she couldn't see herself in a mirror. Judging by men's reactions, she knew she must look stunning enough.

On the fourth night, she set up her equipment at the best spot she'd found, near the rounded end of the bar where there was some unused space. While she was drawing an elderly man who sat in the chair beside her wood easel, Kevin quietly walked up to her.

"Brent Logan just came in," the bartender whispered in her ear. "He and his foreman are at the booth by the far window."

"Thanks," Maisie said, and hurried to finish the caricature she was working on.

After the elderly man gave her five dollars and walked off with his picture, Maisie rose from her chair and took a look across the small restaurant to the far window. There she saw a blond, leathery-faced man in a denim shirt sitting across from another man with graying dark brown hair, whose back was to her.

She stepped behind the bar to ask Kevin, "Which one is Brent Logan?"

"The guy on the right side of the window, facing away from us. The other guy is Clay, his foreman."

Maisie thanked him and grabbed the drawing she'd made of Kevin that he'd framed and set against the wall behind the carved toad. She walked up to the booth by the far window.

The blond man that Kevin identified as Clay saw her approach. He stopped talking to his dinner partner. His weathered gray eyes brightened. "Hey, young lady. Something we can do for you?" He eyed the picture she held by its thin, metal frame.

"My name is Maisie Flowerday. I'm an artist," she explained with a smile. "Kevin was nice enough to give me permission to do caricatures here. Like this one. Just wondering if you'd care to have me draw you?"

"Say, that's a good likeness of Kevin. Isn't it, Brent?" he said, looking at the man across from him.

Maisie turned to Brent, too, taking in his features for the first time. Her mouth dropped open. She gazed at his face, awestruck. His mustache broadened as he gave her a jaunty smile, his teeth big and white. A lock of his dark hair, lightly streaked with gray, fell over his lined, tanned forehead. He had bushy eyebrows that raised whimsically over blue eyes.

Brent chuckled. "Sure is." He gazed up at Maisie and paused a moment, looking captivated. "You should do a painting of yourself."

She laughed. "I'd much rather draw you."

"What do you charge?" he asked with a dimpled grin just as appealing as her favorite movie star ever had.

"I'll do you for free," she said, in a breathy voice. She couldn't help herself and blundered on. "You know, except for your blue eyes, you look an awful lot like Clark Gable. Anyone ever tell you that?"

He stared at her with astonishment. "That old actor? How would a girl like you even know who he was?"

An only child, Maisie had grown up in the fifties and sixties watching Gable movies on TV. She even saw his final movies in theaters. But she couldn't tell Brent that. "Hasn't everyone seen *Gone With the Wind*? I love old movies."

"Must be your new mustache," Clay said, amused.

Brent stroked the thick, stiff hairs above his mouth. "So, you think I look like . . . um, what was his name again? Rhett . . . ?"

"Butler," she replied with glee. "Rhett Butler. You sure do. I always had a big crush on Rhett." What she told him was perfectly true. "You even sound like him. You have that clipped way of speaking. Authoritative and masculine."

"I think you ought to get your portrait drawn," Clay said to Brent with a sly wink. "Go on. I'll keep your cheeseburger safe."

"It'll only take ten minutes or so," Maisie said, looking at Brent eagerly. "And your burger hasn't even been delivered yet."

"Okay," Brent agreed.

"Wonderful. My easel is over by the bar."

Maisie led him to the chair set beside her easel. As he took a seat, she set the framed picture of Kevin on the bar, and sat down in front of her drawing pad. She picked up her black marker and began to sketch. Her subject wasn't any challenge. She'd drawn Clark Gable, just for fun, many times over the decades from old movie magazine photos she'd kept in a scrapbook she'd made as a teenager.

"You want me to pose smiling?" Brent asked. "Or serious?" He seemed to be enjoying watching her work.

"I've already done your smile," she replied. "So just relax."

"You work fast," he commented with surprise.

*You have no idea.* She smothered a giggle. Realizing she'd gotten over-excited at having the spitting image of Gable sitting in front of her, she made the effort to collect herself. She had to remember her purpose. She needed to get to know Brent, to influence him to try to woo back his runaway bride-to-be, Annie, so he would put a wedge between Annie and Rafael.

But as she glanced at Brent again, to capture the manly brightness in his eyes, she began to realize she'd already lost interest in her original purpose. That plan was being eclipsed by a new one taking firm hold in her imagination. She wanted Brent for herself. She could have her own personal version of her long-sighed-over heartthrob, Clark Gable. What would it be like to bed him?

Rafael might be to die for—in fact, she actually had died for him. She'd eagerly let him turn her. But then she'd gotten bored. She wondered, as she sketched, if the same thing wouldn't happen again with Rafael? Despite the vampire sex.

Brent Logan provided her with greener pastures than she'd ever seen. No, she wasn't going to pass up this opportunity!

"So, Brent," she grew a bit breathless saying his name for the first time, "are you married?" She already knew he'd been jilted, but she needed someplace to start a conversation.

"I'm a widower," he said. "My wife died in a car crash several years ago."

Maisie looked up in surprise. She hadn't heard that. "I'm so sorry."

"Thank you. I have a daughter. She's sixteen."

*Well, that puts a dent in my plan.* Maisie managed to hide her disappointment. A daughter at home might hinder Maisie's progress in seducing him. "What's her name?"

"Zoe. She's a handful. Raising her by myself is a challenge," he said. His expression perked up. "She's good at drawing. She'd probably enjoy watching you work."

Maisie's eyes widened as she seized the opportunity he'd just handed her. "I could give her lessons in caricature art," Maisie offered. "I can come over any evening."

"Aren't you working here evenings?"

"Not every night," she quickly replied. "I'm flexible. Whatever evening works best for Zoe, would work for me."

He seemed to be hesitating, thinking.

"I believe it's good for a girl to have a hobby she enjoys," Maisie prattled on, remembering her own youth. "Is Zoe an only child?"

"Yes, she is," Brent replied, looking serious.

"I was, too," Maisie said. "Drawing was a wonderful outlet for me. Kept me happy when I felt lonely. When I was little, I misunderstood the term 'only child.' I thought it was 'lonely child.'" Maisie paused, remembering when she was a little girl, residing in a big house with her parents and a live-in maid, having no one to play with. And the grown-ups, though very caring, were so dull.

Brent's expression grew warm and interested. "Maybe that would be a good idea, teaching Zoe to do caricatures. My daughter sometimes has a waspish sense of humor. Be good if she could take it out on paper in a drawing, instead of giving me and others her snarky remarks."

Maisie chuckled. "She sounds a little like me, when I was her age."

"Frankly, you don't look much older than Zoe," he said.

"Oh, I'm well-preserved," she quipped as she quickly wrote three words below the drawing of him she'd just finished. She unclipped the pad from the easel and tore off the thick sheet of paper she'd worked on. Turning it around to show him, she joked, "You should have said, 'Frankly, *my dear*.' I won't write in the rest of what Rhett told Scarlett at the end of *Gone With The Wind*. Because I think you do 'give a damn.'"

He took the sheet from her and studied it, humor bringing out the dimples in his cheeks again. Just like Gable.

"Frankly, my dear," he murmured, laughing. "You made me look like Rhett, all right. Even put me in a suit with an old-fashioned tie. I'm wearing denim tonight."

"You look fine in denim," she replied. "I can do another of you dressed just as you are."

He shook his head. "I've taken up enough of your time. What do I owe you?"

"I told you, this one's for free. But I'd love to meet Zoe and give her a lesson."

"Okay, sounds good," he readily agreed. "I'll ask her, of course, but I think she'll like the idea. How can I get in touch with you?"

"I'll give you my cell phone number," she told him with enthusiasm. "Call me anytime. Well, that is, any evening. I'm kind of busy during the day." He needn't know yet that she was busy resting in her coffin as long as the sun was in the sky. She took the picture she'd drawn out of his hands for a moment and wrote her phone number on the back.

"It's a deal. Can't wait to show this to Zoe," he said as she returned the caricature. "She'll love it."

"I'm eager to meet her," Maisie told him with great sincerity.

"You're quite a young lady," Brent said. "Beautiful and talented. You make me wish I wasn't forty-eight years old."

"Age is irrelevant to me," she said in an airy tone.

He chuckled and pointed his finger at her. "You could get into trouble telling a man that."

"I trust you," she replied, leaning toward him just so.

"Well, thank you, Maisie." He seemed slightly befuddled. "Goodnight, *my dear*," he told her, giving her a little actor's bow before he headed back to his table.

She watched him as he took long strides in his cowboy boots, just like Gable in *The Misfits* with Marilyn Monroe as his leading lady. Maisie imagined herself as Brent's co-star in real life. Brent had no idea what a pretty pair they were going to make.

*Chapter Four*

Rafael and Annie walked to the stables to take a moonlit ride over the chaparral, something they liked to do together once or twice a week. When they entered the modern, well-kept stable where the Appaloosa horses were kept safely overnight, they found Inez and Francisco visiting Pearl Girl.

After greeting them, Rafael eyed Pearl Girl. The nine-month-old colt was lying comfortably in one corner on a bed of pinewood shavings. The beautiful little horse had a blond mane and tail, contrasting with her light-reddish-brown coat. She had a prominent blanket of speckled white over her rump, a classic Appaloosa characteristic. Rafael had named her Pearl Girl because he thought the white spots looked like pearls on sand.

"She seems very contented," he observed with satisfaction.

"She's doing fine in her own stall," Francisco said. "As you see, she has her own nightlight and a fan going so everything is just right." He glanced at Inez fondly. "Inez has a tendency to spoil her."

"I do not," Inez retorted with a smile as she sat on the shavings next to the colt, nuzzling the young horse's cheek with her nose.

Everyone laughed.

"I may have to train you as well as Pearl Girl," Francisco quipped.

Inez looked up at him. "Just try it."

Again, they all laughed. Rafael looked at Annie and gave her a hug. He enjoyed the camaraderie that had developed between the four of them. He felt in these pleasant moments like a normal man.

"Pearl Girl is already showing a beautiful lateral gait," Francisco said.

"What's that?" Annie asked.

"The legs on the same side of the horse move together," Francisco explained. "It's a distinguishing feature of the Appaloosas. Gives the rider an easy, gliding ride. Sometimes it's called a running walk."

"Spaniards called it *paso fino*," Rafael told them. "Means smooth-gaited. The ancestors of the Appaloosa breed were brought to the New World by the Spanish conquistadors." He glanced at Annie. "Just a little history. Well, we were about to go on out for a ride. Shall we?"

"You bet." Annie nodded goodbye to Francisco and Inez.

After stopping in the tack room for their saddles and bridles, Rafael and Annie were soon out on the desert chaparral under a three-quarter moon. Rafael rode his leopard Appaloosa, Esperanza, a white horse with black spots. Annie had mounted her favorite, a honey-colored older mare with mottled white patches named Marmalade.

"Inez and Francisco seem to be growing closer," Annie said as she rode alongside Rafael.

"I noticed. I'm so glad to see Inez looking really happy. And Francisco, too. Both were alone and now they have each other." Rafael continued to be conscious of the fact that he was the reason she never married.

"Pearl Girl kind of takes the place of the child Inez never had," Annie commented.

Rafael turned his head to look at her. "I suppose you're right."

Annie glanced at him. "Sorry. I didn't mean to remind you . . . make you feel guilty. I know how hard you are trying to compensate for your past with Inez."

"I didn't take it that way. I know you were only making an observation." He reached out to touch Annie's arm. "Don't you still wish you had a family of your own? It's why you almost married Logan, even though you were in love with me."

Annie seemed to make an effort to smile. "I don't think about that anymore. I'm happy with you, and the way things are."

Rafael made a heavy sigh. "If only I were mortal, perhaps you and I could . . . . But as I am, it won't happen. In all the centuries I've been a vampire, and all the women I've been with, none of them has ever gotten pregnant, so far as I know."

"Don't be concerned about that, Rafael. I chose you. I accepted the consequences. To me, it's all been worth it." Her eyes in the moonlight seemed to take on an adoring glow as she reassured him.

Rafael nodded, wondering how he merited a woman who loved him that much.

Annie raised her eyebrows in a playful way. "Speaking of your former paramours, I'm hoping Maisie won't show up again and expect me to 'share' you."

"I'm happy she hasn't reappeared, but I do wonder what she may be up to." Rafael thought back on his brief time living with Maisie. "She's like a perpetual adolescent. I think her parents must not have known how to set boundaries, so she got away with mischief just to see if she could."

"I've had a few students like that," Annie told him. "They're easily bored and not good at focusing, at forming and reaching a goal. They wind up dropping out of college, which is a shame."

"Enough about Maisie," Rafael said. "How is the semester going so far? Good students?"

Annie drew in a long breath. "The students this year are great. They make teaching enjoyable."

Rafael studied her, wishing he could see her expression better in the dim light. "But you seem a little unsettled. What aren't you saying?"

"Oh, nothing to worry about."

"When you say that, it only makes me more concerned." He pulled up on his reins, making Esperanza stop, and reached out to make Marmalade come to a halt. "Tell me."

"You remember Frank Florescu?" Annie began.

"How could I forget? The Romanian professor at your faculty party who recognized I was a vampire. Has he been harassing you?"

Annie drew in a breath. "He called me a 'whore.'"

"What?" Rafael's anger quickly flared.

"He's still furious that I was promoted instead of him. He's positive you're a vampire, and he says . . . well, awful things about the fact that I'm with you." She looked at Rafael. "But everyone in the Archeology Department thinks he's off his rocker, so I'm not worried."

"What can he do to you? Do you need protection? I can hire someone to go to the campus with you."

"No, no." Annie shook her head. "I'm in no danger. I . . . I shouldn't have even told you about it. Never mind. It's okay."

Despite her reassurances, Rafael felt there was more to it than Annie was saying. "You're sure?"

"Yes." She urged her horse to move forward. "Come on, let's ride. It's a beautiful night."

Rafael rode alongside her again in silence, wondering what she wasn't letting on about her encounter with Florescu. He gazed up at the stars, wishing he could pray for her to be kept safe, wishing her life was not troubled by the fact that he was one of the undead. But he felt certain God doesn't listen to a creature existing outside His laws of nature.

# # #

A few evenings later, Maisie drove her RV to Brent Logan's ranch. He'd phoned her the night before to say that Zoe was anxious to meet Maisie and take lessons from her.

Maisie parked in front of Brent's sprawling ranch house, picked up her drawing pad and folded easel, stepped down from the RV, walked to the front door and rang the bell.

She was so eager to see Brent again, she was a bit startled when a teenage girl with short blond hair answered the door. Of course, it was his daughter—the supposed reason Maisie was there. She quickly adjusted her attitude and said, "You must be Zoe."

Zoe grinned. "You must be Maisie! Come in." The girl, dressed in high boots and a mini skirt, opened the door wide. "I loved the picture you made of my dad," she gushed. "Hope you can teach me to draw like that."

"I'll do my best," Maisie said as she walked in. She was also wearing tall boots and a mini skirt. Her red knit top, more demure than usual, had a neckline that did not plunge, yet revealed some cleavage. She noticed Zoe wore a T shirt that fit snugly and emphasized her curves. "You and I have the same taste in clothes," Maisie said, pleased.

"I noticed that, too," Zoe said, laughing. "Love your outfit. Dad thinks I shouldn't be so 'showy.' But I'll be seventeen soon. Why shouldn't I wear what I want?"

"I totally agree," Maisie said. "You're a girl after my own heart." She gave Zoe an on-the-same-wavelength smile which Zoe readily returned. "I like your haircut and the streak of fuchsia."

"Thanks," Zoe said, her blue eyes bright. "Love your long nails. What shade is that?"

"It's my current favorite polish, 'Purple Passion Pink.' So. Where would you like me to set up my easel?"

"How about in the family room," Zoe said. "This way."

As she led Maisie down a short hall into a room with a big couch, some overstuffed chairs and a big, flat-screen TV, Maisie asked, "Your dad home?"

"Yeah. He's in his office on a phone call. He'll probably come down to say hello."

"Good," Maisie said, relieved. Though she didn't mind giving Brent's daughter lessons, beginning her seduction of Brent was her true purpose.

She decided it would work best if she sat on the couch with Zoe, so Zoe could watch her draw. "Can we move the coffee table? I think I'll set up my easel in front of the sofa."

"Sure." Zoe pulled the glass-topped low table out of the way.

Once she had the easel in place, she asked Zoe to sit next to her. "I use a poster marker like this one." She showed the marker to Zoe so she could see the brand name. "It makes a thicker line the harder you press. And a thin line with a light touch." She showed Zoe by drawing on the pad of paper she'd set on the easel. "For shading, I use this." Maisie picked up a small, narrow crayon with a slanted tip. "Use this to show the contours of the face. I'll give these to you and some paper so you can practice."

"Thanks," Zoe said. "Do you begin by drawing the outline of the face?"

"I start by sketching the eyes, then the nose and mouth. Then I add the shape of the chin and then the hair. Turn and look at me, and I'll show you how I'll draw you."

Eyes sparkling with excitement, Zoe did as Maisie asked. Maisie spent a moment studying the girl's face, then began with deft strokes sketching in Zoe's eyes, while Zoe watched.

As she finished drawing Zoe's chin, her father walked in.

"Hey, how are you girls doing?" Brent said.

"She's making a really cool caricature of me," Zoe told him.

"I'm sure she is," Brent said, smiling at Maisie.

Maisie looked up at him with big eyes as he came over to see her sketch. "We're doing great. I'm almost finished. Want to sit down and be a model for Zoe to draw? I'll guide her along."

"Sure. This armchair?"

"Pull it up a little closer," Maisie said, giving him a subtle wink. She made a quick job of sketching in Zoe's short hair, with a bit of shading for the fuchsia streak at Zoe's left temple.

Brent sat down, and Maisie and Zoe switched places at the easel. She tore off the caricature of Zoe, leaving a fresh, blank sheet, then handed Zoe the marker and shading crayon.

"Okay," Maisie said. "Let's start with your dad's handsome eyes. Can't wait till we get to his moustache."

"Yeah, that'll be fun," Zoe agreed as Maisie gave Brent one of her demure yet alluring smiles.

Brent chuckled in exactly the same sardonic way Clark Gable would have. "I can't wait either."

As Zoe began to sketch his eyes, Maisie counseled her to use a lighter touch. But soon she could see that Zoe did have a natural talent, just as Brent had told her.

"Good, Zoe. You've even caught that sexy glint in his eyes."

Zoe turned to look at her with a grin. Brent, however, didn't seem to know where to look.

"Oops, sorry," Maisie said, wishing she hadn't let that slip. "I'm only saying what I see."

"He's free," Zoe said as she continued drawing. "He could use some fun in his life."

"Zoe," Brent chided her.

"Just saying what I see," Zoe replied, imitating Maisie.

Maisie laughed. She was beginning to really like Zoe. And she liked the girl's father even more, in a much different way.

She saw Brent rolling his eyes. Apparently he was not as much of an authority figure in his daughter's life as he'd like to be. Maisie could tell he was the type of man who found women baffling. He'd be putty in her hands. Once she could get him alone.

Which posed a problem. How would she manage that?

# # #

Late one afternoon Annie was helping Inez wash windows at the duplex. They'd finished the windows at the ranch house. Rafael never hired cleaning people. Window spray in hand, Annie listened as Inez confided how Francisco kept courting her.

"So I don't know what to do," Inez said as she rubbed out a spot on her kitchen window. "Francisco doesn't know about Rafael and me. Do you think I should tell him?"

Annie hesitated. "But then you'd probably have to tell him that Rafael is—"

"I know," Inez replied with a worried sigh. "I think, for Rafael's sake, I'd have to go to him before I say anything to Francisco."

"What a dilemma," Annie quietly said.

They were interrupted by a knock at Inez's door. Inez dropped the old linen towel she was using and walked to the living room. Annie watched to see who was at the door. Probably Francisco, Annie guessed.

"Zoe," Inez exclaimed as she let the teenager in. "We haven't seen you in a while."

"Too much homework," Zoe said as she and Inez hugged. "I tried the ranch house, but no one answered. Glad you're home, Inez."

With a smile, Annie walked up to them. "We're house cleaning today. So nice to see you, Zoe."

"Annie, there you are," Zoe said and gave Annie a hug, too. "Miss you guys."

"Want a cold drink?" Inez offered.

"Nah, can't stay long. Dad doesn't know I'm here. No one to keep tabs on me. When he's not home after school's over, I borrow one of our ranch pickup trucks and go where I want."

Inez shook her head. "That wouldn't happen if I was still your cook."

"I know," Zoe said. "I wish you still worked for us, even though I like these opportunities to escape."

Annie felt touched by Zoe's words. Inez had been something of a mother figure for Zoe after Zoe's mom had died. Annie was glad the rebellious teen valued Inez. Zoe had a good heart. The one regret Annie had in not marrying Brent was that she wouldn't be Zoe's stepmother.

"Can you sit with us for a minute?" Inez asked. She motioned to the couch and chairs.

Zoe plopped down on the couch. Inez sat at the other end of the couch, and Annie took an easy chair.

"Guess what?" Zoe said. "I'm taking drawing lessons."

Inez looked pleasantly surprised. "I remember that pencil sketch you did of me last year. It really looked like me. I think studying art is a wonderful idea for you."

"Are the lessons from a teacher at your high school?" Annie asked.

"No, she comes to our house in the evening. Twice a week. She's really good and lots of fun. And . . . ," Zoe glanced at Annie, "she really likes my dad. Says he looks like Clark Gable."

"Clark Gable?" Annie drew her brows together in puzzlement. "I'm not a movie buff, but it never occurred to me that he resembled any actor."

"After you left, he grew a moustache," Zoe said. "Makes him look different. I had trouble getting used to seeing hair on his upper lip. But Maisie is over the moon about him. He seems to like it that she flirts with him. He flirts back!"

"Wait," Annie said, growing alarmed. She glanced at Inez who was leaning forward, looking concerned. "Your drawing teacher is named Maisie? What's her last name?"

"Flowerday. Funny name, huh?"

Annie drew in a long breath, unsure what to say. She saw Inez rubbing her forehead, her eyes grim.

"And she comes over two nights a week?" Annie said. "I would think once a week would be enough, since you have your homework and school activities."

"Well, at first my dad said it would be once a week, but Maisie suggested twice a week."

*I'll bet she did.* "How did you meet her?" Annie asked.

"Dad met her at the Turquoise Toad. He said she sets up her easel there and draws people's caricatures for five dollars. She told me it's a fun hobby, that she doesn't really need the money."

Annie exchanged a knowing glance with Inez. What was Maisie up to? Why had she insinuated herself into Brent's and Zoe's lives?

"Well . . . ," Annie said, at a loss.

Zoe looked at Annie. "I thought you'd like to know that Dad may have a new woman in his life, that he's moved on. And you have Rafael, so everyone's happy. Right?"

Annie nodded. "I'm glad your father has gotten over the cancelled wedding. I hoped he'd move on and find someone new." What she told Zoe was perfectly true. But she hadn't foreseen that he would meet a female vampire.

Annie and Inez chatted with Zoe a while longer about school and an upcoming spring dance. Soon Zoe said she'd better get home before her father did. She gave Annie and Inez hugs and then drove off in the pickup truck she'd borrowed.

Inez closed the door and gave Annie a woeful look. "Does it never end? Dealing with one vampire has been difficult enough."

Annie took hold of Inez's arthritic hands. "And you and I are the only ones who know. Why would Maisie go after Brent? She wanted Rafael for vampire sex. Unless . . . ."

"Oh, don't even think it," Inez said.

"Maisie obviously loves men," Annie said, pondering aloud. "I noticed her making eyes at Francisco that night she came here."

"Oh, my God," Inez murmured, looking at Annie with alarm.

"Don't worry. If she's fixated on Brent now, maybe she won't come back here." Annie raised her eyebrows. "Maybe she'll leave Rafael alone."

"But if she's out to seduce Brent," Inez said, "she may turn him for vampire sex. What happens to Zoe?"

Annie let out a long sigh. "I don't know. Should we ask Rafael?"

*Chapter Five*

The next evening, Maisie rang the doorbell at the Logan ranch house, her easel and art equipment in hand. In a few moments, Brent answered the door, looking surprised.

"Maisie," he said with a smile. "Zoe's at a girlfriend's sleepover tonight. Didn't she tell you?"

She pretended to think about it. "I don't remember her telling me. It's our usual night for a lesson, so I just came over." In fact, she knew perfectly well that Zoe would not be home.

"Oh. Sorry about the mix-up," Brent said.

"That's okay. Since I'm here, I can give you a lesson," she said with a smile.

He looked tempted. "Well, I don't know about a lesson. I can offer you a cup of coffee."

"Thank you," she replied. "It's a little chilly out tonight."

As he opened the door further to let her in, she saw him eyeing her miniscule mini-skirt that covered her rounded bum and not much more, and her ruffled white blouse with its plunging neckline.

"I can imagine you'd be chilly in that outfit," he said with his Gable chuckle.

Maisie was already feeling aroused in anticipation. She set her folded easel against the wall next to the door.

"I'll get the coffee," Brent said, about to go toward the kitchen.

She grabbed his arm. "Why don't you warm me up instead? I'll bet you have lots of body heat. Lend me some."

"Wh-what?"

She leaned up on her tiptoes in her boots, drawing her mouth close to his. "I've been wanting to get close to you ever since I first set eyes on you. You're so handsome and manly."

She kissed him on the mouth, which he resisted for a half-second, and then returned the kiss with energy. His hands slid around her waist.

"Oh, Brent," she breathed, clinging to him with her arms around his neck. "I want you. Is that naughty of me to say? I'm not usually so forward, but I can't stop thinking about you. About what it would be like to . . . you know. If it's just the two of us here tonight, why not?"

His breaths were coming faster, but he pulled away a bit. "I have to think of Zoe. She's a little too interested in boys. I need to set a good example. You're about the most sexy girl I ever met. But I can't—"

"How would she ever find out? I won't tell. You won't tell." Maisie took her hands from around his neck and pulled open the deep V of her blouse, exposing her breasts and her hard nipples. "Why shouldn't we enjoy each other?"

He stared at her voluptuous body, looking as if he were in a sensual daze. "You're unbelievably beautiful."

Maisie smiled. "You can touch. Go ahead." She took his hand and lifted it to her breast, pressing his palm into her flesh. His thumb quickly found her nipple and he teased it, making her gasp. "Ohh, Brent. I'll go crazy if you don't have sex with me this minute." She reached down to feel a strong bulge beneath his zipper. "You want me, too! You can't deny it."

He was breathing heavily now. "I've had dreams about you. Nearly every night. Always X-rated."

Maisie giggled with throaty glee, knowing he craved her, too. "My body is all aquiver." She unzipped his jeans, loosened his garments until she'd freed his erection. "Oooh," she cooed, feeling his hardness with her hand. "This is going to be *so* good."

"The bedroom's upstairs," he said.

"No time for that. I need you this instant. How about here?" She pushed him toward a decorative loveseat in the entryway by the front door. "Sit." She hiked up her tiny skirt, uncovering herself. Panties were such a bother, she never wore them. She climbed astride him and guided him into her, closing her eyes in erotic rapture as she began rocking her pelvis back and forth.

She kissed him as he fondled her breasts, and her rounded derriere. Loving the feel of his rough moustache against her face, enjoying his thick hardness that easily and quickly brought her to a stunning climax, she cried out, "Ohh, Clark. Clark!"

In the throes of his own climax, he seemed to not notice. When the overwhelming sensations subsided, they recovered holding each other.

"You're such a good lover," she whispered. And she meant it. For a mortal, he was one of the best she'd ever had. Not as powerful as she remembered sex with Rafael was, but in this moment she didn't care. The Spanish vampire who had transformed her, to whom she'd returned to reclaim as her lover, had become a fleeting memory. Brent was fulfilling her decades-old dream about her teenage movie star heartthrob. Maisie was in her bliss. And she wanted more of the same.

"You're a fabulous lover," Brent said, still panting, looking as if he was working to regain his senses. "Did you call me Clark?"

"Oh, did I?" She ran her hand through his hair. "I'm sorry. You're even better. My real life, personal heartthrob. Let's do it again, Brent."

He gazed at her, a sincere helplessness in his eyes. "I don't know if I—"

"Of course you can," she cooed reassuringly. "I'll revive you. Where's the bedroom?"

# # #

At around four a.m., Maisie looked at Brent, naked next to her, exhausted and asleep. Over the eight or nine hours they'd been in his bed, she'd been able to coax him into servicing her desires five times—not bad for a middle-aged mortal man. She'd drained him of energy. And now she had a difficult choice to make as she stared at the carotid artery gently pulsing at the side of his neck.

She could leave him as he was, untouched. She could take some of his blood and put him under her power, to have at her beck and call. Or, she could consume some of his blood, then make him drink from her, to turn him into a vampire—something she'd never done. She always liked a man to be under her control. But if she changed Brent into an immortal like herself, she would have her own personal, super-sexed version of Clark Gable. Forever. The very thought aroused her senses.

But then she thought of Zoe. She really liked Brent's daughter. Zoe was like the fun-loving little sister Maisie never had. She realized she felt protective of the girl. An odd feeling. In fact, at their last lesson, Zoe had confided that a boy she liked at school wanted to have sex with her, and he even had a plan of how they could sneak off and "do it." Maisie had astonished herself by counseling the girl to wait, not jump into bed so quickly, advising Zoe that at sixteen boys could take advantage and disrespect her. Maisie had begun sneaking off to sleep with boys when she was fifteen. When had she become so conservative?

And now she was considering how having a vampire for a father would impact Zoe. She'd only be able to see him at night. He'd have to have a coffin hidden somewhere. Zoe was likely to discover it. How would he explain it all to her? How would a young girl be able to deal with such a situation, and such a secret? Who would be around during the day to give her guidance, make sure she went to school and kept up her grades? No one.

For perhaps the first time, Maisie found herself worrying about someone else. What an annoyance, but she couldn't help it. She wanted Zoe to have a proper upbringing.

Therefore, Maisie realized she had to rule out turning Brent into a vampire. Maybe when Zoe was all grown up and out of the house, Maisie could feel free to transform him.

So that left two possible ways to go: Leave Brent as he was, or put him under her power.

Leave him be? That didn't sound like much fun. Mortal men could sometimes have a mind of their own despite her expert feminine wiles. So that meant there really was nothing more to think about. She would take his blood, and then she would have a mental bond with him. Whenever she wanted Brent, he would have no choice but to comply with her every wish. And he would have his normal daytime life, so there would be no negative impact on Zoe. He'd go on parenting her as usual.

Smiling now that she'd come to a good decision, even proud of herself for doing right by Zoe, she moved closer to Brent as he lay on his back, still sound asleep. This was the fun part. She'd particularly enjoy taking Brent's blood. Gently climbing on top of him, she shifted his head to one side, giving her better access to his carotid. In his sleep, his arms automatically enfolded her and he sighed contentedly. The embrace touched Maisie, made her feel warm and tender toward him. *Am I falling in love?* She wasn't sure what love felt like. Her lips met the pulsing artery of his throat. She gently punctured his skin with her incisors, deep enough to pierce his carotid. He jerked a bit, so she dug her hand into his hair to keep him still, and she began to drink. His blood, hot from his body, tasted rich and wonderful. So much more delicious than drinking from a cold blood bag. She whimpered with pleasure as she drank, and drank. Soon his arms slipped away from her body.

All at once she stopped, growing alarmed. Had she taken too much? His body had begun to feel limp and inert. She drew back and looked at his face. Red streaked down his neck, but his face looked pale. Too pale.

*Oh, no!* She quickly set her fingers just beneath the side of his chin, looking for a pulse. There was one, but it was very weak.

"Brent!" She tried shaking him by the shoulders, but he did not respond.

What should she do? She couldn't call an ambulance. How would she explain the two puncture wounds on his neck? There was no way she could risk revealing herself as an immortal. But she had to save Brent. He'd already become the most special lover she'd ever had.

Looking around the room, she spotted his cell phone on the bed stand. If she could get hold of Rafael, he might know what to do. But she didn't have his number. An idea occurred to her. She picked up the cell phone and looked through Brent's entries until she found what she was looking for. Annie's number. She dialed it.

Maisie grew panicky as she listened to ring after ring with no response. Finally, she heard a woman's voice.

"Hello?"

"Annie?"

"Who's this?" Annie's voice was sleepy and annoyed.

"Maisie Flowerday. I need to talk to Rafael."

"No, you don't." Annie sounded angry now.

"It's an emergency. It's not for me. It's for Brent."

"Brent?"

"I took his blood. He's not responding. Maybe Rafael will know what to do. Can't let Brent die."

"Oh, my God," Maisie heard Annie exclaim. "Rafael, it's Maisie."

All at once Rafael was on the phone. "What have you done?"

"I didn't turn Brent, only initiated him. His blood was beautiful, and I took too much. He's pale and limp. Won't wake up."

"We'll drive over. If he comes to, give him some water to drink."

"Okay. Hurry!" She set the phone down. Realizing she was naked, Maisie put on her clothes. She pulled a sheet over Brent, up to his waist. In ten minutes, she heard the motor of a pickup outside. She rushed downstairs and opened the front door to Annie and Rafael.

Rafael glowered at her. "How can you be so irresponsible? Where is he?"

"In the bedroom. This way." Maisie led them up the stairs.

All three walked into the room. Annie gasped when she saw Brent lying unconscious.

Rafael walked to the bed and bent over him, taking his wrist to find a pulse. "How much did you drink?" he asked Maisie.

"A lot. I'm full. His blood was so good."

Annie looked at her. "Can you wipe your mouth? It's all over your face," she said with revulsion.

"Sorry." Maisie went into the attached bathroom and wet a towel to wipe the blood off her face. She couldn't see herself in the mirror and could only hope she got it all.

She came back to find that they'd placed a pillow under Brent's legs. Rafael was massaging Brent's shoulders while Annie looked on, her face taut with concern.

"Did his eyelids flicker just now?" Annie asked, looking on as Rafael continued trying to revive him.

"I think so. Brent! Wake up." Rafael shook him a bit.

"Huh? Wh-what . . . ." Brent opened his eyes and looked up at Rafael. "Who are you?"

"Rafael de la Vega."

"Why . . . ? What's going on?" Brent seemed to try to sit up, but couldn't.

"He's okay!" Maisie exclaimed with relief.

"Maisie, get some water," Rafael ordered.

"Maisie . . . Maisie and I made love," Brent said dreamily.

"I doubt it was love," Rafael muttered. "Overwrought sex is more like it."

"It was love," Maisie said, giving Rafael a glass of water. "I really care for him. Will he be all right?"

"I hope so, no thanks to you," Rafael replied. "Annie, I'll lift him to sit up. See if you can get him to drink some of this." He handed the glass to Annie. "His body should be able to replace lost blood cells, but he needs fluid."

"Right," Annie said. "Thank goodness he's reviving."

Rafael changed positions to sit on the bed in back of Brent and supported him to sit up. Annie put the glass to his mouth, and Brent took some sips.

"What happened?" Brent asked again. He looked down at his chest. "Where is this blood coming from?" A trickle had run down from the punctures in his throat.

Annie looked at Rafael and then at Maisie. "What are you going to tell him?"

"The truth, unfortunately," Rafael replied. "It's the only way. He needs to understand the situation Maisie has put him in." He shifted his harsh eyes to Maisie. "Do you have to seduce every man you meet? He has a young daughter."

"Is Zoe asleep in her room?" Annie asked.

"She's on a sleepover with a friend," Maisie said. "Of course I wouldn't have done this if she was home."

"Why did you do it at all?" Rafael asked. "What were you thinking? Can't you confine yourself to men who are unattached? You are so damned irresponsible."

"And you are *so* mean!" Maisie retorted. "I wanted to turn him. But I remembered Zoe, and that it wouldn't be good for her to have a vampire for a father. So I only initiated him. I *did* do the responsible thing."

"The responsible choice would have been to not take his blood at all," Rafael shot back.

"But I need him. I didn't want to risk losing him," Maisie tried to explain.

"Why? You have your way with other men and then ditch them. What's so special about Brent?" Rafael asked.

"He's just like my favorite movie star, Clark Gable. I've had a crush on Gable forever. Brent is like my dream man. He's what I've always wanted. And now he's mine."

Annie was shaking her head, looking incredulous as she continued to hold the glass to Brent's lips as he sipped. But then Brent lifted his hand haphazardly to push the glass away.

"What are you all talking about?" Brent asked.

Maisie, Rafael and Annie were silent for a long moment.

Rafael grabbed a pillow from the other side of the bed and propped it up behind Brent. He stood and faced Brent. "Do you believe in vampires?"

"Huh? No, of course not."

"Well, you've been bitten by one. Maisie is a vampire. And so am I."

Annie took hold of Brent's wrist. "It's true, Brent. I didn't believe it when I first met Rafael. This will take a while for you to fully understand."

"Maisie bit me?" Brent lifted his hand to the side of his throat. He looked at the blood on his fingertips. "Why?"

"Because you and I are so good together," Maisie said, stepping closer to the bed. She sent him a mental wave of unity. His eyes widened. "See? We're closer than ever now. We have a bond. I can communicate with you wherever you are."

He looked at her with puppy dog eyes. "You're wonderful. You're really a vampire?"

Maisie smiled at him. "I'm an immortal. And you belong to me now."

While Brent looked at her with adoration, from the corner of her eye, Maisie could see Rafael wincing in consternation. She turned to him.

"How can you take the moral high ground?" she asked. "You've initiated women. You did it to me without asking."

Rafael lowered his gaze. "Yes, I did, and have regretted it. I've tried to evolve, Maisie. I don't take anyone's blood anymore. Annie is untouched because I love her too much to defile her. Maybe someday you'll evolve, too. Meanwhile, you and Brent will have to figure out how to keep your new bond a secret from Zoe. She's too young to have to learn her father is the slave of a female vamp."

Maisie stuck out her chin. "Zoe won't know. I can manage to keep my relationship with Brent secret."

"Like you've managed this?" Rafael said with scorn. "You might have killed him. If you love his blood that much, you'd better not drink from him again."

Maisie reluctantly nodded, pretending to agree with Rafael only so he would stop scolding her. What did she ever see in Rafael? She looked at him and then Annie. Assuming a polite tone, she said, "Thank you for coming. For reviving him."

Annie glanced at her wristwatch. "It's about an hour before dawn. Time you and Rafael need to retire."

"Maisie can stay here," Brent said, looking puzzled.

Maisie bowed her head. "No, I can't. I'll see you tomorrow night and explain it all." She took note of the wounds she'd made on his neck, no longer bleeding profusely, but still fresh. "Wash the blood away," she told him. "Wear a bandana or a scarf to cover the marks. No one should see them." She sent him a mental message to ensure he understood.

"Okay," he said. "I will."

For a moment, Maisie felt bad that she'd changed his life and left him her wounded slave. But then she thought of the nights she'd spend with him, after Zoe was asleep, of course. And she decided feeling guilty was stupid.

*Chapter Six*

Rafael sat fuming in the passenger seat as Annie drove the pickup truck back to Rancho de la Noche. He'd taken an abandoned old dirt road across the desert to get to the Logan Ranch as fast as possible. Annie was driving the longer way home down paved roads. Good thing she was there to take over the wheel for their return trip. Rafael was so blindly angry he was liable to run them into a Saguaro cactus if he were driving.

"What did I ever see in her?" He asked the question of himself more than Annie. "Look at the damage I've caused because I was foolish enough to turn her!"

"Don't blame yourself," Annie said in a soothing tone. "How could you know this would happen all these years later?"

He shifted in his seat. "I suppose you're right. At least she's no longer fixated on me." He looked at Annie. "You don't have to worry that she's a threat to our relationship."

"That's maybe the one good thing that's come of this," Annie agreed. "For us. It's a worry, though, that the new woman in Brent's life is Maisie. I'd be happy for him to move on and forget me, but not with a flighty creature like her." She glanced at Rafael. "Do you think they can keep what's happened a secret from Zoe?"

Rafael shook his head. "I don't know. Inez was able to keep her bond with me secret for decades. But I never went to the Logan Ranch. I called Inez to come to me. Maisie is already at their ranch regularly. Zoe's not stupid. She'll soon figure out something's odd."

Annie turned the truck into the driveway of Rancho de la Noche. "But Zoe likes Maisie. I can see how they might be kindred spirits. Both are rebellious. They dress similarly. Maisie's giving her drawing lessons. Zoe probably looks up to her, maybe even sees her as a role model."

"Don't tell me anymore," Rafael said as Annie came to a stop in front of the ranch house and turned off the ignition. "It only makes me furious. I need to run, let off some steam."

"As a wolf?"

"It's the only way I can feel free. Let go."

"Is there time? Dawn is coming."

He smiled indulgently at her. "Don't worry, I instinctively know when the sun will rise. There's time for a quick run. And then I can rest more easily."

She nodded and he kissed her, thankful that she was so understanding of something that was beyond comprehension for most mortals. He got out of the truck, went into the house, took off his clothes and changed into wolf form. He bolted out the back door, across the corral, jumping a fence, able to run so much faster on four legs. With the cool night air on his snout and furry ears, he felt liberated, free of trying to remain human, free to live in the moment, to let go of the cares that burdened him.

Changing into a wolf was an aspect of his vampire nature that he appreciated, that helped him cope with being one of the undead. If he hadn't had moments like these, running wild under the moon and stars, he didn't know how he could have kept his sanity over the last four centuries.

Fortunately, now he also had Annie to confide in and love. What would he do without her?

# # #

The next day, in the early afternoon, Annie knocked on Inez's door.

"Come in," Inez said with a smile. "I'm just cleaning up lunch dishes in the kitchen."

"I'll help." Annie followed Inez to the kitchen. "I thought I should tell you what happened at the Logan Ranch.

"Something happened?" Inez picked up a dish towel at the sink.

"Here, I'll wipe." Annie took the towel from her and picked up a rinsed mug. "Remember Zoe told us Maisie was giving her drawing lessons? Well, last night Zoe stayed at a friend's house, and Maisie seduced Brent."

"Oh, no—"

Annie told her everything.

Inez sank into a chair at her small kitchen table. "I knew Maisie would be trouble. Zoe's always been a handful. With Maisie controlling her father, she'll be completely under Maisie's influence."

Annie had finished wiping the dishes and sat down at the table with Inez. "What can be done? Neither of us has any sway with Brent anymore."

Inez tilted her head in a doleful way. "The vampire bond is very strong. When Rafael called me to him with his mind, there was nothing I could do. I had to go. It's hard to describe to someone who hasn't experienced it. I knew it was wrong, but he pulled me to him. It almost seemed like I was in a trance when he summoned me. And yet I loved him." She closed her eyes for a moment. "Even now, I still admire him even though he's let our bond lapse. I respect him because of the way he's changed." She looked fondly at Annie. "Since he met you, he's become more honorable. He puts doing what's right above satiating his needs."

Annie sighed, feeling her own adoration for Rafael. "He so wants to be mortal again." She sniffed. "Something I doubt Maisie will ever wish for."

"Thank you for telling me," Inez said, "though it's not something I'm happy to hear." She paused and swallowed, then looked at Annie intently. "I'm glad you came over, because there's something I've been wondering . . . worrying about, lately."

"What?"

"Francisco. He really likes me. Silly man." Inez smiled, but then her expression grew serious again. "I think—not sure, of course—but he may even ask me to marry him."

Annie's heart swelled. "It's obvious he's smitten with you. That would be wonderful for you both. Wouldn't it?"

"But, Annie, I have a past."

"Does Francisco need to know?"

"Shouldn't a marriage be based on honesty?" Inez asked. "I told you about the time, long ago, that Francisco drove me home after I'd spent the night with Rafael. So far, Francisco doesn't seem to have put it together that I'm that mortified girl he took home. But what if he does? He thinks it's remarkable that Rafael gave me Pearl Girl. What if Francisco somehow finds out *why* Rafael gave me such a generous gift?"

Annie thought this over. "I suppose it is best to be honest. But then you'd have to reveal that Rafael is a vampire. Francisco doesn't know, does he?"

"It's pretty obvious he doesn't. And that's why I think I should talk to Rafael. Ask if he minds that I confess everything to Francisco. He may object, but I have to ask. It's so difficult to tell Francisco how I feel when I have this shameful secret."

"So, you do have feelings for him?" Annie asked in a delicate way.

Inez hesitated. "Yes," she said in a small voice with a doting smile. "He's a wonderful, kind and sweet man. Nice looking, too. What's not to love?"

Annie gave Inez a reassuring hug. "Then talk to Rafael. I'll go with you, if you want."

# # #

That evening Annie sat with Inez on the couch in Rafael's living room while he listened intently from an armchair. It quickly became clear to Annie that she had to do most of the talking, as Inez had apparently become tongue-tied.

"So," Annie finished, "Inez feels she needs to tell Francisco about her past. Which means your true nature would probably have to be revealed. Otherwise, how could Francisco understand why she would have continued in a secret affair for so long? Especially when she's very religious."

Rafael nodded that he took her point, but appeared unsettled. "I don't see why Francisco needs to learn all about her past. What he doesn't know won't hurt him."

Inez leaned forward stiffly. "I just worry he might find out some other way. When Brent fired me, right away you offered me a job and a place to live. You even gave me Pearl Girl. He knows you give me special treatment and he must wonder why. He might put it together that I'm the girl he drove home when my horse ran off. It's better to tell him everything now, so he won't be shocked if he finds out after I'm his wife. Francisco is a fine man. I want to be fair to him. Or I'd feel like I was marrying him under false pretenses."

Rafael sat back in his chair and rubbed his eyes. "It's a marvel he hasn't guessed there's something terribly abnormal about me. All these years I've considered whether I should tell him what I am. But I've always feared losing the best horse trainer in the state, and my longtime colleague. I've never had many friends."

Inez nodded and bowed her head. "I'm sorry to ask this of you."

Rafael turned to her. "You wouldn't be in this situation if it weren't for me. I want you to be happy. I mustn't stand in your way." He drew in a long breath and let it out. "All right. High time Francisco learned the truth. But how will he take the news?"

"He's a level-headed, easygoing person," Annie said, trying to keep hope alive as Inez and Rafael seemed to sink into apprehension. "He may be astonished at first, but he cares about both of you."

"Astonished?" Rafael repeated with grim amusement. "Horrified is a better word."

"I think he'll be shocked to the core," Inez said, her expression intent and her voice sounding like she was trying to be brave.

"When will you tell him?" Annie asked.

"The sooner the better," Inez said softly.

Rafael glanced at the clock on the fireplace mantel. "He'll be coming over in a few minutes to update me on our Appaloosas," Rafael said, resignation in his tone. "I don't want this confrontation weighing me down. Shall we get it over with and tell him tonight?"

Inez nodded, looking scared. "I hope he doesn't hate me," she whispered.

Rafael dug his fingers into his thick black hair. "He'll hate *me* the most. I've lied to him for decades. What will he think when he finds out his boss is a vampire who once seduced the woman he'd like to marry?" He shook his head. "This won't go well."

Annie clasped her cold hands together tightly, growing anxious, too. "But he's patient and kind. It may take a while, but he'll forgive you." She said this with more conviction than she felt.

Rafael gave Annie an admiring stare. "Thank God for you. Of the three of us here, you're the only normal one. The fact that you choose to love us may lend us a veil of decency."

Inez turned to her with beseeching eyes. "Rafael is right. If Francisco sees that you haven't turned your back on Rafael or me, even though you know everything, he may be more accepting."

"Sure," Annie readily agreed. "I'll be happy to support you." She smiled, but her stomach began to tighten. All of a sudden, a lot seemed to rest on her shoulders. She hoped she didn't fail them by not finding the right words or tone to keep Francisco from overreacting.

Yet Annie had to admit to herself that if Francisco didn't feel duped and angry, he'd be nothing less than a saint.

# # #

Rafael felt a jolt of doom when he heard Francisco's knock at his door. He looked at Inez, then Annie in a questioning way. Both nodded grimly. With their unspoken approval to go ahead with their plan, Rafael answered the door.

Francisco walked in with his usual sunny smile. Though his eyes did not quite meet Rafael's, as had become his custom the last several years. Rafael knew Francisco must sense, perhaps even unconsciously, that Rafael could mess with his mind when their eyes met.

Heading toward the office, Francisco paused when he noticed Inez in the living room with Annie. He looked surprised and pleased. "Hey, Inez. Annie."

"Hello." Inez appeared to try to smile, but couldn't seem to manage it.

"Something wrong?" Francisco asked.

"Would you sit with us?" Rafael said. "We need to tell you something. Ranch business can wait."

"Sure." Concern in his eyes, Francisco walked to a leather armchair, nervously straightening the collar of his denim shirt as he sat down. "What's going on?"

Rafael drew in a long breath as he sat opposite Francisco. How could he explain the unexplainable? He gazed at the horse trainer's kind, weather-worn face and felt deep remorse. "There's no other way to say this, except to get to the point. What do you think about the existence of vampires, Francisco?"

"Vampires?" He laughed. "I watched the old movies on TV when I was a kid."

"I mean, in real life," Rafael explained. "There are books and movies, but vampires are more than popular folklore. They are present in the real world."

Francisco looked perplexed. "Um . . . okay. So . . . ?"

Annie spoke up, repeating what she'd so recently told Brent. "When I first learned vampires were real, I was taken aback, too."

"So," Rafael said, picking up on Francisco's unexpressed question, "I have something I've kept secret for decades that I must reveal to you."

"What? That you're a vampire?" Francisco asked with a jittery chuckle. "Come on. What's this all about?"

"I am a vampire." Rafael stated the truth directly, wishing he could be anywhere else but here facing Francisco.

"No. How can you say that?" Francisco seemed perturbed now. He glanced at Inez.

"It's true," Inez assured him, tears standing in her eyes.

Rafael leaned forward. "You've never seen me in the daytime."

"You told me your eyes are sensitive to light," Francisco said.

"I made that up," Rafael confessed. "I lied to you, and I'm sorry. There's a secret underground room below the kitchen. During the day I rest there.

In my coffin. And sometimes in the kiva at the ancient ruin."

Francisco rubbed his forehead with a shaking hand. "This is a little hard to take in."

"Telling you my dark secret is hard for me, too. I admire and respect you. I greatly fear that you will no longer respect me." Rafael bowed his head for a moment, but then continued. "I can read men's minds. And control their thoughts. I can make them forget if needed. It's with great regret I have to confess that I've manipulated you in that way."

Francisco suddenly met his eyes squarely. "There have been spaces of time I couldn't remember. I wondered what was wrong with me."

"That was my doing. I suspect it's why you don't like to meet my eyes anymore. You sense I can interfere with your thoughts. I promise you I won't ever do that again. In fact, I haven't for some time."

"What have you made me forget?" Francisco asked with alarm.

"Times you've seen me with a woman, saw the marks on her neck. Once you saw me transform into a wolf."

"A wolf?"

"The black wolf you and I once talked about," Inez said. "The wolf that rescued the child and brought him back to the reservation. The Indians believe he's a wolf spirit. That was Rafael."

"I've seen him change form," Annie said. "It's one of his vampire powers."

"I have superior strength, too," Rafael added. "Years ago when your duplex was being built, the daytime workmen didn't secure a roof beam properly.

That night as we looked over their work, the beam came down and almost fell on you. I was able to catch it in time. But you were so surprised at my strength and agility, I had to make you forget the incident."

Francisco's expression had grown mystified and wary. "I have no memory of that. I do recall the workmen fixing the fallen beam. What did you say about marks on a woman's neck? You mean you drink blood, like in the movies?"

Rafael found it uncomfortable to meet Francisco's eyes. "I'd put women under my power that way, so they'd keep my secret. And for their blood. I get blood from blood banks now. Don't ask how. All you need to know is that I no longer bite anyone. Annie, as you see, is untouched."

Annie pulled aside the collar of her blouse, while Inez worriedly chewed her lip.

"I'm trying to be better. It's taken me far, far too long to override my vampire urges. I'm working to become as fully human as I can." Rafael poured out his deepest feelings. "I would give anything to be a mortal again."

"You're not mortal," Francisco said with new understanding. "That's why you don't age."

"Right."

Francisco nodded slowly, still looking confused. "But why did you have to tell me all this? I was happy not knowing that you've lied to me all these years, that you can get into my head and rearrange my thoughts."

"Because I didn't want to keep secrets from you anymore," Rafael said. He glanced at Inez. "And because it seems you've grown fond of Inez."

Francisco looked at him sharply. "What's Inez got to do with it?"

"She was the young woman you saw me with one night, outdoors, impetuously taking her blood. You saw her neck bleeding. I had to make you forget. One night when I called her to me, she found in the morning that her horse had run off. You drove her back to the Logan ranch. She told me about it the next night, and I had to make you forget that, too."

Francisco looked at Inez, wide-eyed. "Is that true?"

A tear ran down Inez's cheek as she nodded her head.

"You were coming to see Rafael in the night?" Francisco repeated, incredulous.

"It wasn't her fault," Rafael hastened to say. "I first met her at the ruin one evening. I'd been resting in the kiva and found her there at sunset. She was quite young and very pretty. I was a cad. I seduced her. Took her blood. I put her under my power to ensure that she wouldn't tell anyone. Through the mental bond I created with her when I drank from her, I continued to call her to come to me."

Francisco grew pale, looking thunderstruck. "How long did this go on?"

Inez seemed to find her voice, though it shook as she said, "Thirty years. He let me go about fifteen years ago. Rafael knew that I was religious, and that I worried more and more about my immortal soul."

"Why, what was your sin?" Francisco asked. "Giving him your blood?"

Inez wet her lips, as if her mouth had grown dry. "Not only that. I was his mistress."

Annie laid her hand on Inez's arm. "Rafael had her under his control. She couldn't end the relationship."

"It was wrong of me," Rafael said as he saw anger rise in Francisco's eyes. "Unforgiveable. I was lonely. She was quiet and good, not like other women I'd met. I grew fond of her. Didn't want to let her go. Finally, my conscience caught up with me. I could see how much I was making her suffer, because she believed she was sinning. But she had no choice. The sin is on me, not her. God must have forgiven her, and I hope you can overlook it, too."

Francisco said nothing. Rafael felt at a loss as to what more he could do. He glanced at Inez, whose eyes were red with tears and hopelessness.

"It's because Inez has grown fond of you," Rafael explained, "and you seem to like her, that we thought it best to tell you all this now. Not wait until your attachment with Inez has grown even stronger."

Inez seemed to find her voice again. "I wanted to be honest with you, Francisco. Because of my past, I've been afraid to return your feelings. If you can't accept me now, I understand perfectly."

Francisco stared straight ahead, looking increasingly pale. Inez got up from the couch and went to him.

"Are you all right?" Inez asked. She set her hand on his shoulder.

He flinched.

Inez drew back, as if he'd slapped her. "I'm so sorry."

"Are you going into shock?" Annie asked, rising from the couch. She felt Francisco's hand, though he quickly shook her off. "You're cold and clammy. I'll make you some tea," she said, as she hurried toward the kitchen.

Inez awkwardly sat down again, looking stricken.

Rafael rose and got down on one knee beside Francisco's chair. "You aren't going to pass out, are you? You're perfectly safe. Nothing has to change. I value you most highly and hope that in time you can forgive me. And above all, that you can forgive Inez. I'm revealing my dreadful secret to you, putting myself at risk. I won't make you forget, and I'm trusting that you won't betray me. You're an honest man, and I wish to be one, too."

Annie came back holding a steaming mug with the string of a tea bag hanging out of it. She went to Francisco's side as Rafael rose and stepped away. "Take some sips of this."

Francisco looked annoyed but did as she asked.

"I was shocked when I first learned all this, too," Annie told him. "But I've come to love Rafael. He was the victim of a gypsy curse centuries ago, when he came over here as a Spanish conquistador. He hates what he is. He's tried to make amends with Inez. It's why he gave her Pearl Girl. And let her have a home here. She's become my best friend. I've never met a more honest and caring woman."

Rafael was relieved to see some color come back into Francisco's face. Though Francisco seemed to listen impassively to Annie's heartfelt words.

Annie sat on the couch again with Inez. Rafael sighed as he took his seat again. He waited a few minutes, waiting for some response from Francisco.

"Do you have anything to say?" Rafael finally asked.

Francisco set the mug down on the coffee table and rubbed his eyes. "I hoped this was all just a nightmare. That I'd wake up. But I'm awake, and either all this is true, or you people are crazy. Well then, this is what I have to say. I can't work here anymore. Can't deal with this. I'll be out of here in the morning."

"No!" Rafael exclaimed, mortified. "Please don't go. The ranch would fall apart without you. You're irreplaceable. We may be flawed, but we all love you."

Inez began openly weeping into her hands. Francisco glanced at her, but then looked away.

"Please reconsider," Annie said, slipping her arm around Inez's shoulders.

"Nothing to think about," Francisco said, his eyes stark. "I can't be here anymore. How can I trust you people? Never in my life thought I'd be lied to about vampire secrets. I feel weird just sitting here with you."

Inez wiped away tears. "I understand, Francisco. It's all right. I believe it's my punishment to go through life alone."

Rafael saw Francisco lower his gaze. Turning to Inez, Rafael told her, "It's because of my ill-spent youth that I wound up being cursed. You got caught up in my vampire existence without knowing it."

Rafael faced Francisco again. "Won't you at least take a few days to think this over? You've been here for so long. What would our Appaloosas do without you? Won't you stay a while, if only for the sake of the horses you love so much?"

Francisco's eyes coldly met Rafael's. "I'll stay until a new trainer is found to replace me. And don't worry. I won't spill the beans that you're a vampire. Who would want to work here if they knew that!"

*Chapter 7*

"I'm going to ask Brent if I can have my old job back," Inez told Annie the next morning as Inez put away washed breakfast dishes from the oatmeal and eggs she'd cooked for the Rancho de la Noche ranch hands.

"Really?" Annie sounded dismayed. She had stopped by to talk and started helping sort clean spoons and forks into their slots in a kitchen drawer.

"I can't stay here," Inez explained, feeling weighed down by her reluctant decision. But she'd recovered her lifelong stoicism to accept what was. "I thought about it all night. This morning when I served the men breakfast, Francisco wouldn't even look at me."

"But he said he wants to leave. If he goes, can't you stay?" Annie asked.

Inez lifted her shoulders. "If I'm not here anymore, maybe he might keep his job. He's not young. Would another rancher hire him? I think he might come to tolerate the idea of working for Rafael. They only see each other for a while in the evening. But me . . . I don't think he'll ever be able to look upon me as he used to. He wouldn't want to have to run into me every day. If I go, he might feel more comfortable about staying. And then he could continue working here until he retires. It's better for him if I go."

Annie didn't look happy, but seemed to understand Inez's reasoning. "The men here will miss your cooking. Do you think Brent would take you back?" Before Inez could reply, she added, "Actually, now that he's under Maisie's power, maybe he would. He'd understand what it was like for you to be under Rafael's spell, why you helped me run away with Rafael."

Inez nodded in agreement. "Brent said I was disloyal. And I was. If I show Brent the scars on my neck, tell him I was Rafael's mistress, don't you think he'd understand how, even now, I would do anything for Rafael?"

Annie's eyes widened. "You mean you still feel his power over you? He shut down his mental bond with you, didn't he?"

"He did. But the memory of that bond stays with me. When I saw him again, that night before your wedding when he came to claim you, that old yearning to make him happy came upon me again. And I wanted you to be happy, too. How could Brent have ever replaced Rafael in your life?"

Annie smiled. "No, he couldn't. But Maisie sure seems enamored with him."

"That's another thing. I worry about Zoe. Maybe I can be a steadying influence for her."

"But will you be safe?" Annie furrowed her brow. "Couldn't Maisie bite you? Then she'd have you and Brent under her control."

Inez pondered this. "I don't know. It didn't occur to me."

"Does wearing a cross work?" Annie asked. "Like in the movies?"

Inez shook her head. "I wore a small silver cross when I first met Rafael at the ruin. Didn't seem to bother him one bit."

"Oh." Annie lowered her eyes in thought, but then she looked at Inez. "How about if you go to the Logan Ranch during the day, so you're there for Zoe before and after school, then come back here before sunset? That way you won't encounter Maisie."

"And I'd be out of Francisco's way most of the time," Inez said. "It might work. I'll go over there and talk to Brent today. I hope Rafael won't mind."

"Rafael only wants the best for you." Annie glanced at her watch. "I need to go. I have classes today, and it's a long drive. Hope all this works out for the best for you and everyone."

Inez made an effort to smile. "I'll get out my rosary."

# # #

Inez waited until late afternoon to go to the Logan Ranch, figuring Zoe would be home from school by then. When she rang the doorbell, Zoe answered.

"Inez!" Zoe opened the door wide to let her in and gave her a hug. "It's great to see you."

"I've missed you," Inez said as Zoe closed the door. "You look cute." She eyed Zoe's leather miniskirt and sweater.

"Maisie let me borrow her skirt. She looked so fabulous in it."

"How nice of her," Inez said, hiding her dismay. "Is Maisie still giving you drawing lessons?"

"Yeah, but between you and me, I think she's really coming over to see my dad," Zoe said in a bright, confidential tone. "They just seem to be nuts about each other. He's like a lovesick puppy with her."

"Well, I've come over hoping to talk to him. Is he home?"

"He's upstairs in his office," Zoe replied. "Is he still mad at you? I'll try to soften him up. Why do you want to talk to him?"

Inez hesitated. "I'm hoping he might let me come back here. Not as a live-in cook. But so someone will be here to make you a good breakfast and give you a nice snack when you come home from school. Maybe even an early dinner. Who's been cooking for you?"

"That would be great," Zoe exclaimed. "Dad hired a caterer who brings in dinner for us and the ranch hands. We all fend for ourselves for breakfast and lunch."

"I see. Maybe you could go to your dad and ask if he's willing to speak to me," Inez said.

"You bet." Zoe immediately ran upstairs.

Inez waited by the door. Without Brent's permission, she was reluctant to go any further into the house in which she'd lived for most of her life. She wondered what his reaction would be.

In a few minutes, Zoe called from the top of the steps, "He'll see you. Come on up."

Inez climbed the stairs and paused at the open door of his office. Brent looked up from behind his desk, dressed casually in a chambray shirt. Inez took note of the bandana around his neck.

"Now, Dad, be nice," Zoe told him. "We need Inez back."

Brent gave his daughter a nod. "Go do your homework."

Zoe left and Inez slowly approached Brent's desk.

He leaned back in his chair, no hint of a smile on his face. "Zoe says you want your old job back."

"I'm hoping you'll consider it," Inez told him politely. "I don't wish to live here. But I've worried about Zoe, if she's eating properly."

"I heard you got hired by de la Vega."

"I did. But I hoped I might work here, part time."

Brent looked a bit perplexed. "Why should I take you back? You helped my bride-to-be run out on me."

Inez walked back to the door, closed it, then stepped up to the desk again. "Brent, I know what's happened to you, why you're wearing that bandana. You never used to wear one."

His expression changed and his eyes grew wary.

Inez pointed to the two small scars at the side of her neck. "I was once under Rafael's power. And I know the truth about your new romance with Maisie Flowerday. You're not just smitten with her, you're bonded with her and it's a bond you can't fight."

"You, with Rafael?" Brent said, astonished.

"From the time I was nineteen. He finally let me go. But even so, I couldn't stand in the way of his happiness. Annie loves him and he loves her. I didn't want to be disloyal to you, but they were meant for each other. You can't fight Maisie, nor do you ever dream of wanting to. I understand what you feel, the oppressive yearning you have to be with her, to please her."

Brent looked stricken. "It's true. I worship her."

Inez nodded, remembering how she used to feel toward Rafael. "I worry about Zoe, and Maisie's influence on her."

"Maisie wouldn't hurt Zoe. As Zoe puts it, they're BFFs."

"But is she a good role model?" Inez asked. "I've met her. Maisie is such a free spirit, seductive and oversexed."

"You don't have to tell me," Brent said with a sigh of exhaustion. "She wears me out."

Inez looked away. "So, I thought if I was here, I might be a steadying influence. I love Zoe, like the granddaughter I never had."

"But don't you cook for the Rancho de la Noche people?"

"That's not working out so well. They have fewer workers who live on the ranch than you do. They don't need me. But Rafael will let me keep the home there that he's given me. To make up for the large part of my life I devoted to him, as you are giving of your life to Maisie."

Brent's eyes widened, perhaps only now fully realizing the impact Maisie was having on him and his world. He gazed at Inez with a shaken expression. "I think it would be good for Zoe if you came back. I'll pay you the same as before you left. Okay?"

Inez smiled with relief. "Thank you, Brent."

*Chapter 8*

A few days later, on the weekend, Annie took the opportunity to continue her work at the remote Anasazi site on the edge of Logan property. Rafael rested in the kiva as he had when she first encountered him. She looked forward to dusk, when he would arise, and they would make love there, just as they did when they first met.

It was about three p.m., as Annie took archeological notes sitting on a low wall of the sandstone ruin, that she thought she heard the motor of a pickup truck in the distance. In the quiet desert atmosphere, the sound of a motor was out of place with the wind blowing through the cottonwood trees in the valley below, or the sound of flapping wings as a crow flew by. She wondered if it might be one of Brent's ranch hands looking for stray cattle. Several minutes went by, and soon she heard footsteps on the plateau above the cliff which contained the broad cave in which the ancient people had built their home.

She grew distracted, wondering who it was, then alarmed when she saw a man hiking down the steep path that led to the edge of the ruin. She set down her notes and pulled her backpack closer. The gun Brent had given her when she first started excavating the ruin was still in her pack. She'd forgotten to return it. He'd given it to her for safety, since she worked alone at the ruin. She hoped she wouldn't need it now.

As the man got closer, she recognized him. Frank Florescu. What was he doing here?

She rose to greet him, warily. "Frank. Hello."

"Dr. Carmichael. Wasn't easy to find this place."

Annie drew her brows together. "I'm working. Come to spy on me?"

He lifted his shoulders in a blasé shrug. "Just want to see the site that got you so much recognition. Nice dig you've provided for the Archeology department. Eventually I may bring students here to learn hands-on excavation, just as you will."

She nodded and smiled a bit, covering her suspicion that he was still hoping to find something to discredit her.

"Feel free to look around," she said. "It's a great little site. You'll see I've discovered a collection of black and white pots that I've left in place for now. Some still contain grains of corn. Mano and metate, too. I even found a sandal, but I have that at home."

Florescu looked around the ancient, small Anasazi dwellings with aloof interest, as if to show he'd seen better ruins in his career. He paused when he noticed the low, broad, round structure dug into the sandstone ledge in front of the crumbling pueblo rooms.

"The kiva is in surprisingly good condition," he said. "Have you gone inside?"

Annie worked to appear nonchalant. "Yes. It's empty."

"Ladder still intact?"

"No," she lied.

"I think I'll take a look. Kivas were off limits for the Indian women folk. That's why I like them."

"I told you, there's nothing to see," she admonished. "It's just a typical kiva."

Ignoring her, he slid the flat stone aside that covered the entrance. "There's a ladder here," he said. "Why did you say there wasn't?"

"It's not firm," she said, grabbing his arm to pull him back. "You might get hurt."

He pulled his arm out of her grasp and peered down into the darkness. "Looks in great shape to me. Like new, in fact." He pulled a keychain out of his pocket that had a small flashlight attached and pressed the button to turn on the light. "I'm going in."

"No!"

"Why?" he said as he turned to climb down the ladder. "Something here you don't want me to see?"

Fearing for Rafael, who was helpless and might even be harmed by the sunlight being admitted into the kiva, Annie knew she had to do something. Florescu was about to discover him. She hurried to her backpack and took out the revolver Brent had given her. Tucking the gun into the waistband of her jeans, she rushed back to the kiva and descended down the ladder.

She found Florescu shining the beam of his small flashlight over Rafael, who weakly turned his head away from the shaft of sunlight pouring through the opening above, just missing contact with his body.

"He *is* a vampire!" Florescu exclaimed. "You lied!"

"I lied to protect him," Annie said. "I love him."

"What kind of woman are you?" Florescu said with disgust. He looked up at the sunlight pouring through the hole above them. "I'm going to end this right now. I'll pull him into the light. Should be interesting. I've never seen a vampire turn to dust."

Annie took the gun out of her belt and held it on the professor. "Don't touch him or I'll shoot you."

Florescu took a step back. "Do you even know how to use that?"

"I once shot a wolf with it." She cocked the gun to further intimidate him. "You're not nearly as scary."

She was relieved to see that he apparently was not terribly brave.

"Okay," he said, backing away another step. "Keep calm. I won't touch him."

Annie wet her lips. "We need to leave. But before we do, I want you to look at the helmet and armor over there. Shine your light on it."

Florescu looked in the direction she indicated and shifted the beam of his flashlight. He grew curious. "That's a Spanish helmet."

"Exactly right. Rafael was a conquistador who came over with Coronado's men. He was born in Salamanca and before he left Spain, a gypsy put a curse on him. On his thirtieth birthday, here on the Arizona desert, he was bitten by a wolf in the night. He died, the men buried him, and later he dug his way out of the shallow grave. The gypsy curse had turned him into a vampire." She looked at Florescu squarely. "It's not his fault that he became one. He'd do anything to be mortal again. Can't you try to have some compassion for him?"

"He's an evil, undead creature," Florescu said. "Doesn't matter how he got that way."

"And you're a heartless, pitiless man," Annie said, seething with contempt. "Rafael is far more human than you are. Get out of here." She shoved the revolver in his face. "Now!"

"Okay, I'm going. Quit waving that gun around." He headed toward the ladder and climbed it. She kept the gun on him until he reached the top, then followed him. When both were at the top, she pointed the weapon at him and said, "Push that slab back over the opening."

Florescu did as she asked, sliding it back into place.

"Thank you," she said. "Now go."

"I'll tell our colleagues what I saw," Florescu asserted in a blustering tone. "I'll have you drummed out of the University."

"And who would believe you?" Annie countered. "They already think you're nutty for believing in vampires. Your tactic to discredit me didn't work before and it won't work now."

"The evidence is there in the kiva!" he exclaimed.

"Rafael has another place to rest. Now that you've discovered this place, he won't return to it. We'll remove the armor. You can bring anyone you want here. They won't find any trace of a vampire, and you'll look all the more foolish."

Looking demolished, he stood there impotently for a moment. But soon anger burned in his eyes. "I'll find a way. You haven't got the best of me yet!"

He turned and headed toward the path that led up to the plateau above. She kept her gun on him until he moved out of sight. In a while she heard the distant sound of a motor starting and a vehicle driving away.

When she felt sure Florescu was gone, she found her flashlight and climbed back down into the kiva, sliding the cover back over the opening to preserve the darkness. Using her flashlight, she walked to where Rafael lay dormant, resting on a blanket. She set the flashlight on the ground, away from his face, and took his hand. His eyes fluttered open.

"Everything's okay," she told him. "I'll stay with you until sunset."

Looking peaceful, he closed his eyes. Annie reclined next to him, her head on his shoulder. She took the flashlight in her hand and turned off the light. There in the deep darkness she imagined what it must be like to exist as Rafael did. How could he have coped, in all his hundreds of years, never seeing the sun?

Later, at dusk, Rafael began to stir. Annie had fallen asleep, and his movement woke her up. She turned on the flashlight she'd kept in her hand.

"What happened?" Rafael asked, sitting up. "Someone was here with you."

Annie shifted to sit facing him. "Florescu. He came to see the ruin. I had no idea. I tried to stop him from going down here, but couldn't. When he discovered you, I got the gun and held it on him. He was going to pull you into the sunlight."

"To destroy me," Rafael murmured. He looked at Annie with adoration. "You saved me."

"Thank goodness he's a coward. I was afraid I'd have to shoot him. I showed him your armor and told him your story, hoping he'd have some compassion. But—"

"He had none. I remember fragments of what he said."

"He's still threatening to do something. I saw malevolence in his eyes. You won't be able to rest here anymore, Rafael. And we'll have to hide your armor somewhere."

"We'll take it with us now. I'll keep it in the room with my coffin."

Annie nodded with a heavy sigh. "Let's go. I don't feel safe here."

*Chapter 9*

Around three a.m., seeing Brent had fallen asleep next to her in bed, Maisie began to draw languid circles around his nipple. They'd enjoyed their third go-round for the night, and she wanted more. She rubbed her naked thigh over his and stroked her hand slowly downward over his belly button and below.

"Brent, wake up," she softly urged. He looked so tired. She decided he didn't really need to wake up as long as she could coax another erection from him.

But all at once his eyes opened. "Huh? Oh . . .no, Maisie." He stopped her hand from fondling him. "I'm exhausted. Have some pity."

Maisie drew back, looking at him while she let her naked breast flatten against his bare shoulder. "But we're having so much fun. I love our nights together."

"I do, too, Maisie. But I'm a middle-aged man. We went at it all night last night. I'm too worn out to oversee my ranch and attend to business. And what about Zoe? I wanted to be a good role model, but she knows you stay the night with me."

"So she thinks we're having an affair," Maisie said. "It's not unusual for a single dad to have a girlfriend."

"I don't want her to use my behavior as an excuse to start having sex with boys."

"I told her to wait," Maisie said. "She confides in me. I told her a boy could take advantage of her that way."

Brent sat up against his pillow. "You did?"

"Sure. I started sleeping with boys too young. I don't want her to make that mistake. I like her. I want her to . . . to live a good life." Maisie found herself saying words that amazed her. "I've always been energized living on the edge. Since becoming an immortal, it's easy and natural for me to exist this way." She felt puzzled by her own feelings. "But for some reason I don't want Zoe to be like me."

"Absolutely not," Brent said. "I don't want her to be promiscuous or to be drawn into . . . into this vampire life of blood and obsessive sex."

"She won't know about that, I promise," Maisie said.

Brent's eyes darkened with worry. "My bandana slipped. She saw the marks. I told her I cut myself shaving. I'm not sure she bought that explanation."

"I can make her forget," Maisie said.

"Are you going to keep making her forget things she shouldn't see or know?" Brent asked. "She's very inquisitive. Notices everything."

Maisie stroked his forehead. "You worry too much."

Brent looked at her with intense lights in his blue eyes. "Remember what Rafael said—Zoe's too young to have to learn her father is the slave of a female vampire."

Maisie used her mental bond with him to send calming vibes. "Rafael makes a tragedy out of everything. Never mind him. This is between you and me. We'll keep Zoe safe from our secret." She kissed his cheek, then his mouth, pressing her breasts into his chest. He began to respond, enfolding her in his arms. "I need you just once more," she whispered. "Then I'll go and let you sleep. Okay?"

"Okay," he said.

Maybe it wasn't fair. She knew Brent was helpless to refuse her. But she wanted him to indulge her, to fulfill her magnificent desire for him. Of all the mortal men she'd had, Brent was the best. The very best. He fulfilled her old dream of bedding her movie star heartthrob.

And she'd come to appreciate Brent for himself. In the throes of passion she hardly ever called him Clark anymore.

# # #

The following Wednesday, Inez drove back to Rancho de la Noche in the late afternoon to spend a little time with Pearl Girl, before driving back to the Logan's to cook dinner. That morning she'd made a good breakfast for Zoe, Brent, and the ranch hands at the Logan spread. She'd been working there for a few days now and things seemed to be going well. Though Brent looked so haggard, with dark circles under his eyes, she worried about him.

Inez parked the pick-up in front of her duplex. She would have liked to see Annie, but knew that Wednesdays she taught classes at the University. Inez walked to the corral where the young Appaloosas had room to wander. Inez's pace quickened when Pearl Girl saw her and stepped toward the wooden fence to greet her.

It was then that Inez noticed Francisco coming out of the stables. She hadn't spoken to him, in fact had avoided running into him, in the week that had passed since Rafael had told him everything. As she began to stroke Pearl Girl's nose over the fence, she saw Francisco take notice of her, then quickly look away. Her heart sank, but she understood. She concentrated on giving the colt her full attention.

Then, to her surprise, she heard footsteps and turned to see Francisco approaching her. His face, however, looked like a grim mask.

"Hello, Francisco."

"Inez." He nodded to her. "Pearl Girl's doing well. I think she missed you."

"She looks fine. I can see she's grown."

Both fell silent. Inez couldn't think of what more to say to him, so she continued to focus her attention on the colt. She was relieved to see that Francisco seemed calm, at least, and that he was willing to speak to her.

She snuck a glance at him. He seemed involved in his own thoughts.

But in a moment, he took a long breath, set one hand on the fence, and said, "I'm sorry, but I'm having a hard time accepting everything you and Rafael told me. Even the idea that vampires are real."

"Will you continue as Rafael's trainer?" she asked.

"For the time being. I don't know what to do. I don't like to be around him, knowing he had me fooled all these years. Don't like that he lied, and how stupid I feel that he managed to dupe me." He let go of the fence and straightened his posture. "And hardest of all is to accept that you had a . . . a past with him. It makes you seem like a different person. Maybe it wasn't your fault. He made you submit. But still . . . ." He drew in a shaky breath. "I don't like to be an unforgiving man, but it's hard to wrap my mind around it."

Inez closed her eyes tightly to stave off tears. Pulling herself together, she said, "It's a dreadful secret. I didn't want to go on with us growing more and more friendly, and you not knowing. I had to accept that you would see me differently. So, it's okay. I don't expect you to be warmhearted toward me the way you were. I believe it's my fate, that God wants me to be on my own. Given my past, how could it be otherwise?"

His brown eyes met hers and wavered for a moment. Then he simply nodded and walked away. As a tear ran down Inez's cheek, she opened the gate and entered the corral. She walked up to Pearl Girl and hugged the little horse. It felt good to have something warm and alive to cling to, an innocent creature that would never judge her.

After twenty minutes or more with Pearl Girl, Inez realized it was time to go back to the Logan Ranch and start preparing dinner. She gave the colt a last hug, left the corral and walked back to the pick-up she'd borrowed. But out of the corner of her eye, she saw something moving. She turned to see a tall man, a stranger she'd never laid eyes on, peering into the front window of Rafael's house. She was about to ask what he wanted when she noticed something in his hand.

A wooden stake.

Shocked, she quietly walked back toward the corral at the side of the house, putting herself out of his view. Quickly, she moved as softly as she could to the stables. She thought that Francisco had gone back there. She found him tending to a horse that probably had a limp, because he was examining its hind leg.

"Francisco," she whispered. "There's a stranger sneaking up to Rafael's house, looking in his front window. I don't think he saw me. He's got a stake in his hand."

"A stake?" Francisco looked confused as he rose to stand beside the horse.

"A stake through the heart is how to destroy a vampire." She hoped Francisco would do something. "Rafael is resting. He's helpless if this man manages to break in and find him. It'll be twenty minutes before any police can get here."

Francisco's eyes sharpened. "I'll get my rifle."

He hurried out of the stables to his side of the duplex. Inez waited outside, and in a moment Francisco appeared, weapon in hand.

Inez followed as he took the lead, walking stealthily to the front of Rafael's house. He looked around the corner, then at Inez, shaking his head to indicate no one was there.

"Maybe he's gone around the side," she whispered.

She continued to trail Francisco as he made his way across the driveway, past the front door and window to the far corner. He stopped and peered around it as Inez held her breath. With a sudden alertness, he stepped back, motioning to Inez to stay where she was.

"He's there?" she mouthed.

Francisco nodded. He lifted the rifle to his shoulder and turned the corner. "Hey!" he yelled.

"Get away from that window!" He stepped forward, aiming the gun, and moved out of Inez's view.

Unable to keep to Francisco's instruction to stay back, she crept forward and peeked around the corner of the house. She saw Francisco approach the tall, slim man who appeared startled and scared as he looked down the barrel of Francisco's rifle.

"I'm just trying to see if anyone's home," the man said in an innocent tone.

"Why do you have that stake in your hand?" Francisco asked.

"This?" The man threw it onto the ground. "It's just a piece of wood."

"Looks like it's been whittled down to a sharp point," Francisco replied. Still holding the gun on the man, Francisco slowly moved around him. "Walk back to the front of the house," he ordered. "If you make a break for it, I'll shoot."

"Okay, okay." The man headed toward the front.

Inez got out of the way as he turned the corner, Francisco right behind him.

"Inez, go back and pick up the stake he dropped."

She nodded and began heading toward the side of the house. "What will you do with him?"

"Take him to my place. Hold him there till the cops come."

Inez ran toward the dining room window at the side of the house and found the stake on the ground. She picked it up and hurried back, walking behind Francisco as he forced the man to move toward the door of Francisco's home.

When they reached his small porch, she climbed the two steps ahead of them and opened the front door.

"Don't call the cops," the man kept saying. "I meant no harm. I'm a respected university professor. A colleague of Annie Carmichael. Just came to visit. I thought she might be home."

Inez and Francisco exchanged glances.

"She mentioned to me that there was a professor who was making trouble," Inez told Francisco.

Francisco pulled out a wooden chair from his small kitchen table and set it in the living room. "Sit down," he instructed the man. "What's your name?"

"I don't need to give you my name," he said indignantly, though with the gun on him he complied and sat on the chair.

"Inez, there's an old bandana in my closet," Francisco said.

"I'll get it." She set the wooden stake on the coffee table. Francisco's place was configured similar to her side of the duplex, so she knew she'd find his closet just inside his bedroom door. There she spotted a red bandana tucked into a corner of the top shelf. She brought it to Francisco.

"Tie his hands behind him," Francisco told her.

While she did so, tying a tight knot around the man's wrists, Francisco pointed the barrel of the rifle at the man's head.

"Say your name, or we'll pull out your wallet and find identification."

"I'm Dr. Frank Florescu," he proclaimed. "Professor of Archeology. Just like Annie."

"If you work with her, then you must know her class schedule," Inez said. "She's teaching today. You knew she wouldn't be home."

"Why are you here, peering in windows with a stake in your hand?" Francisco asked. "How did you get here? I don't see any car or truck that might belong to you."

Florescu hesitated, sweat forming a sheen on his forehead. "I wanted to surprise her. Left my truck up by the main highway and walked the driveway."

"I don't believe you," Francisco said. "You're trespassing, and you were attempting to break and enter. Inez, call the sheriff."

Thinking that Rafael might somehow be discovered, she hesitated, but then pulled her cell phone out of her denim shirt pocket.

"Wait!" Florescu objected. "You'll ruin my career."

"Should have thought of that before," Francisco said.

Inez reluctantly began dialing 911.

Eyeing her with anger, Florescu shouted, "I'll tell the cops de la Vega's a vampire."

The cell phone at her ear was ringing, but Inez promptly ended the call and looked at Francisco. "Annie will be home soon. Let's let her decide what to do."

Francisco appeared startled by Florescu's threat. He drew in a breath and nodded, then stared at the professor with contempt. "Looks like you'll be our guest for a while." Keeping his rifle at the ready, he sat on the armrest of his living room couch.

Inez took a seat in the middle of the couch. Like Francisco, she stared at the trespasser, wondering what this was all about. Annie had mentioned there was a professor who was making trouble for her. Something about him losing a promotion to her. Inez had sensed Annie had more reason to be concerned than just that, but she didn't seem to feel like talking about it. Now Inez understood Annie's worry. Florescu had learned Rafael's secret. Bringing the sheriff into this situation might not be the best idea, even though they had caught the professor red-handed.

From the nervous way Florescu darted his eyes back and forth, he appeared to be thinking of some scheme to get out of the mess he'd created. "You two work here for de la Vega?"

"I do," Francisco answered.

"Then you know your boss is one of the blood-sucking undead?"

Inez put on a bold front. "Don't be ridiculous."

Florescu seemed unfazed. "He's a vampire. I saw him lying in the kiva during daylight hours, helpless as a corpse."

Inez's hands grew cold with anxiety, realizing her bluff wouldn't work. "And that's why you came with a stake—to destroy him."

"My family's from Romania," Florescu said with pride. "My father had a cousin taken by a vampire. I know what must be done."

Francisco looked uneasy. "Have you ever actually staked a vampire?"

The professor straightened his posture. "No. But it's my duty."

"A stake through the heart? Like in the movies?" Francisco said. "Sounds bloody. The law officers would come after you for murder."

"I doubt you'd convince the sheriff that vampires are real," Inez said. "They'd lock you in jail or put you in a mental ward."

Florescu looked increasingly pale as they argued with him, yet kept his belligerent demeanor.

"Despite what he is, Rafael is a good person," Inez told him. "I brought him to an old Indian shaman in hopes the shaman could cure him. But when we got there, we discovered the man had passed away. Rafael was devastated. He'd so hoped to be cured."

Florescu seemed to take in this information with doubtful surprise. "An Indian medicine man might have cured him? Really?"

Inez felt encouraged that Florescu was showing a hint of curiosity. "Years ago, this shaman told Rafael and me that he had a ritual he believed could make Rafael mortal again. But Rafael worried he might perish in the process. The shaman agreed there was a risk. So Rafael didn't go through with it. But a few months ago, he changed his mind. Only it was too late, the shaman had passed on."

The professor listened with deep intensity in his hazel eyes, brows knit together. "I've made a private study of vampirism, and I've never heard of this Indian ritual. Is there another medicine man who could do it?"

"Not that I know of," Inez replied. "Why? I thought you wanted Rafael gone."

Florescu seemed to grow uncomfortable with his hands tied behind his back, and squirmed in his chair.

"Academic interest. There's an old Romanian gypsy cure I know of. Wondered if your medicine man used similar herbs, prepared the same way."

Inez drew her head back in amazement. "There's a cure in Romania?"

Francisco, who had quietly listened to their interchange, spoke up. "But he doesn't want Rafael cured." He looked at Florescu. "You came to stake him, not offer a remedy."

"Right," Florescu affirmed, his expression turning dour and angry again.

The three sat in silence. Inez's brief glimmer of hope that there was a cure for Rafael was quashed.

All at once, she heard the sound of a vehicle pulling up on the gravel driveway outside. "That must be Annie."

Inez rose and looked out the door. She saw Annie getting out of her car in front of Rafael's house and hurried toward her.

"Annie," she called, growing short of breath as she ran. "That professor you know is here. Florescu."

Inez told her all that had happened.

Annie listened with a look of startled disbelief. "Oh, my God!" she exclaimed as they rushed to Francisco's. "I can't believe he'd actually come here to stake Rafael."

"We hoped you'd know what to do," Inez said, breathing hard from exertion and anxiety as they stepped up onto Francisco's small porch.

Annie's face had grown tense with apprehension. "Frank Florescu has no respect for me." She looked at her wristwatch. "The sun sets in twenty minutes or so."

Inez intuited Annie's train of thought. "Wait for Rafael?"

"He needs to know. It's his property and his secret. I'll see what Florescu has to say to me. At sunset, I'll go get Rafael."

When they entered Francisco's living room, Francisco looked relieved to see Annie. He continued to hold his rifle at the ready.

Annie approached Florescu and looked down at him with puzzled contempt as he squirmed in his chair.

Inez picked up the sturdy, sharp, wooden stake from the coffee table and showed it to Annie. "He had this in his hand."

With a heavy sigh, Annie gave Florescu an exasperated look. "Have you gone completely off your rocker? Don't you understand your actions can mean the end of your career at the University?"

"Of course, I do." His tone was full of disdain. "A vampire must be destroyed no matter the consequences. It's my duty to my family, to the world."

"You sure have grandiose ideas," Annie said. "Tied up in this chair at gunpoint, you don't look like much of a Van Helsing."

He did not reply, but sat fuming in silence.

"Rafael poses no danger to the world," Annie argued. "You're ruining yourself for nothing."

Florescu swallowed, pressing his mouth into a grim, flat line as a bead of sweat ran down his cheek.

"Is this to get back at me, because I got promoted ahead of you?" Annie asked. "Maybe you'll be promoted next. Our colleagues talk about what a brilliant student you were years ago in grad school. Obviously you have potential. Why ruin it with these kind of antics that only make you look completely insane?"

"If I can't make my mark in archeology, I'll do it some other way," he said in a superior manner. "I'll let the world know that vampires exist and show how they must be destroyed."

"So you've decided to find fame as a vampire hunter?" Annie said. "Who would believe you?"

"People in rural parts of Eastern Europe know the truth. They've encountered the undead. I'll make the world believe."

"From a prison cell?" Annie's tone was laden with sarcasm.

Florescu wouldn't look at her. He tilted his head and seemed to find no reply.

Inez glanced at Annie, impressed that Annie might be making some headway arguing common sense into Florescu. Then she had a thought.

"If you know of a cure," Inez told him, "you might get recognition by healing vampires instead of destroying them."

Florescu grew still for a moment, as if her idea took him off guard.

"A cure?" Annie said.

Inez nodded. "He told us about a vampire cure in Romania."

Annie looked mystified. "Well, if that's true, then you could be a local hero in Romania," Annie told him, her tone tinged with amusement. "What is this cure?"

He sniffed with derision. "Like I would tell you."

Annie sighed again. "The sun has almost set. I'll bring Rafael." She looked at Florescu. "Think you'll be such a brave vampire hunter when he gets here?"

# # #

Rafael climbed the steep steps from his subterranean refuge, the small room below the kitchen where he kept his coffin, wondering if Annie had come home yet. He unlocked the door hidden in the kitchen pantry and found Annie waiting there.

"Rafael." She fell against him and hugged him around the neck. "Florescu's here. He came with a stake."

Keeping his arm around her to reassure her, Rafael listened with astonished dismay as she told him what had happened before sunset.

"Francisco's holding a rifle on him," Annie said. "Florescu says he'll tell the police about you if we have him arrested."

"I can make him forget," Rafael said, thinking it through, "if I can force him to look in my eyes."

"Can you erase his obsession with vampires?" Annie asked. "He believes it's his duty to the world to destroy you and others like you."

"I can erase a memory," Rafael said. "Never tried nullifying a man's life mission."

"What'll we do?" Annie asked, worry in her voice and eyes.

"We'll figure it out," he told her. But he wasn't sure how.

They ran to Francisco's. Inez, watching for them through the window, let them in.

Upon seeing Rafael, Francisco stood, keeping his rifle trained on Florescu. "Inez, show Rafael the stake."

Inez brought the foot-and-a-half-long, wooden stake to Rafael.

"Inez spotted him peeping in your front window," Francisco said. "I got my rifle and found him trying to open a dining room window. Would have called the cops, but . . . ."

Rafael couldn't help but be grateful and heartened that Francisco had done all he could to protect him. He walked up to Francisco and set his hand on his shoulder. "Thank you. You've saved me."

Rafael turned to Florescu, who seemed surprised at Rafael's interaction with Francisco. "And what do you have to say for yourself?"

Florescu sat in silence for a long moment, looking at the floor. But then he raised his head, without meeting Rafael's eyes, and asked, "Were you really a Spanish conquistador?"

This was not any sort of reply Rafael expected. "I was. Why?"

"It's . . . interesting. I'm an archeologist. I like history. And you lived it."

"I did," Rafael said, beginning to be amused. "You want to interview me now, instead of stake me?" He held up the whittled wood and touched its sharp point. "Looks like you meant business. This would certainly have gone through me."

Florescu wet his lips. "Maybe you and I can make a deal."

"A deal?" Rafael almost laughed. "You've aroused my curiosity."

"I know of an arcane gypsy cure for vampirism. I can get it for you, if you don't report me to the sheriff." Florescu's eyes darted to Rafael's face, then looked forward again. "I've heard from a Romanian herbalist that it works. She says she's cured two vampires. They became normal human mortals again."

"A gypsy cure?" Rafael repeated with hesitance and wonder. He set the stake down on the low table, his senses quickening with the possibility that this could be true. "It was a gypsy's curse that made me this way."

"Don't trust him," Francisco said.

Annie caught Rafael's arm. "Frank talked about a cure earlier."

Inez added, "I told him you'd gone to the Indian shaman."

"Right," Florescu said. "I wondered how the medicine man would have done it. If he knew the same herb formula that I've heard about."

"The shaman said it was a sacred ritual," Inez corrected him. "I don't know if he used herbs."

"Too bad he died," Florescu said. "I would have liked to talk to him."

"But you've shown such hatred and loathing for Rafael," Annie argued. "Why are you interested in a cure?"

"He's bargaining so we won't have him arrested," Francisco warned.

Florescu made an effort to sit up straighter in his chair. "Okay, okay, I don't want you to turn me in.

But now that I know more about you, Rafael, I can see you have value. You don't attack people. You have loyal friends. You were a conquistador. And . . . ," he glanced at Inez, "this lady came up with an idea. Instead of trying to destroy vampires, I could cure them. She's right, this might be a whole new avenue for my academic career. I could research this remedy and write a paper."

Annie shook her head in a doubtful manner. "Who would publish it?"

"Not here in the States. I'd go to Romania. Find a position at a university there. I've been quietly researching vampires and vampire lore for years, as a sideline to my archeological work."

"You mean, you'd leave Arizona?" Annie asked.

"Why not? Things haven't gone well for me here. I'm thinking maybe my true calling is to study vampirism in Eastern Europe. My parents came from Romania and I grew up speaking the language. I can easily fit in over there and do the work that most interests me."

"And Rafael would be your first guinea pig?" Annie asked, distrust in her tone.

Rafael looked at her, not understanding.

"Scientists do experiments in labs on guinea pigs," she quietly explained.

Rafael turned to Florescu. "So I'd have to trust you to do this experiment on me. Have you ever yourself seen a vampire cured in this way?"

"No, not with my own eyes," Florescu admitted. "But I have faith in my sources."

"Why should Rafael believe anything you say?" Francisco interjected. He turned to Rafael with an imploring look. "Why don't you just make him forget? It worked with me. Make him forget he ever came here. We'll leave him off wherever he parked his car and let him go. And he won't be the wiser."

"No, don't do that!" Florescu fiercely objected, his hands writhing in the bandana tied around his wrists.

Rafael paused for a long moment, thinking. "If I erase his memory, he might eventually rediscover I'm a vampire. We'd have to go through all this again. Besides, I'm intrigued by this cure of his."

"It's not mine," Florescu explained. He seemed to temper his anger by taking on an even-toned, informative demeanor. "An aunt, my father's youngest sister in Romania, knows this elderly woman named Celestina who is an herbalist. Celestina's a revered great-grandmother, a good woman. People go to her for natural cures for their ailments. My aunt mentioned to her that her nephew, me, was interested in vampires. Celestina said she could cure them, that she learned how many years ago from an aged gypsy woman. My aunt put me in touch with Celestina. I talked with her on the phone once. Before I ever encountered you, Rafael. She assured me she had cured two vampires, said that she would swear on the Bible and by all her beloved icons that this was true."

"Then why didn't you tell me about this cure?" Rafael asked with impatience. "Instead, you threatened me and now you're here with a stake."

The professor glanced awkwardly at Annie. "Because I was insulted that Annie got promoted instead of me. She's too young, a woman, and she doesn't deserve it. When I discovered her new boyfriend was a vampire, I wanted to use that against her, to bring her down. But since Americans think vampires exist only in movies, no one believed me. In my rage and humiliation, I decided to get revenge on Annie by destroying you. I've never staked a vampire, so I rationalized it as research."

He made an exasperated expression as he looked squarely at Annie. "Okay, I admit that envy has gotten the better of me. Maybe you're right, Annie—I've gone off the deep end." After a hesitation, he added, "I'm sorry."

Slowly, fearfully, he shifted his gaze to Rafael. "I apologize to you, too. I know you have the ability to look in my eyes and see that I'm sincere." His voice shook. "As an act of good faith, I'm taking the risk that you won't make me forget. Or sink your teeth into me to put me under your power."

Rafael delved into the professor's widened, wary eyes, into his mind. The man's thoughts were in a swirl, convoluted, frightened and passionate. But he could read that Florescu had formed a new intention, a desire to put himself on a different life path.

"I do see you're sincere," Rafael acknowledged.

"Please don't make me forget," Florescu begged, still meeting Rafael's gaze. "Or bite me."

"I won't. You have my word," Rafael said in an authoritative, formal manner, full of gravity and fate. "We're both taking the risk to trust each other."

Florescu's eyes brightened with relief. "I'll call Celestina tonight and ask her to express mail me her herb formula. As soon as I receive it, I'll bring it to you."

"Alright," Rafael agreed. He looked at the others and saw worry and apprehension in the eyes of Francisco, Inez, and especially Annie.

"Are you sure?" Annie asked him.

"Yes. And now we need to let him go. You can put down the rifle, Francisco. Inez, please untie his hands." Rafael turned to Annie and slipped his arm around her. "I know you don't trust him, but I can see he's sincere. I need to try this gypsy cure."

As Inez untied his hands, Florescu said to Rafael, "I have one request. I want to be there when you take the cure."

"To see if it works or if I perish?" Rafael nodded with gallows humor. "Be my guest."

"I believe it will work," the professor said, rising from the chair. With hesitance he extended his hand. "This will be a unique opportunity for me. For my work. And I promise you that when I write my paper about the event, I'll keep your identity secret."

Rafael took his hand and looked in his eyes. "I'll take you at your word."

Florescu left, assuring Rafael he'd let Annie know when the special herbs from Eastern Europe arrived. After watching the professor go and closing Francisco's front door, Rafael turned to see the long faces on the three mortals in the world he most cherished.

"Please, no gloom and doom," he told them. "I need to do this. You all know how I long to be one of you. I need your support."

Annie quietly walked up to him, hugged his arm and laid her head on his shoulder.

"We support you," Inez said with glistening eyes. "But you can't stop us from worrying we might lose you."

Rafael smiled. "You're a marvel of goodness, Inez. After all I've done to alter your life, I should think you'd be happy to lose me." He looked at Francisco, standing next to Inez in the middle of the room. "Thank you, Francisco, for going to such lengths to protect me from an intruder. I don't deserve such loyalty in return for all the dishonesty I've shown you."

"I didn't hesitate for even a second," Francisco said, seeming surprised at himself. "Despite everything, I had to prevent a guy with a stake from harming you." He glanced at Inez. "I found myself worried Inez might get hurt, too. I had to do something."

She nodded. "He made me stay back while he went to capture Florescu."

"We're grateful for your quick action, Francisco," Rafael said. "Perhaps there's hope that one day you can forgive Inez for the past she endured because of me?"

Francisco nodded, a warm gleam in his eyes. "I still care about you both too much to let the past cloud my feelings." He turned to Inez. "You were brave to tell me everything."

Tears filled Inez's eyes. "Thank you."

"But I'm not forgiving you," Francisco said as he playfully gave her long braid a tug. "There's nothing to forgive." He slipped his arm around her shoulders in a gentle hug.

Rafael glanced at Annie as she leaned against him. "You see? A happy ending."

Annie sniffed back tears. "Happy for them. Hope the ending is the same for us," she whispered. "What'll I do if you don't survive the cure?"

Rafael hated himself for having no good answer to give his beloved.

*Chapter 10*

A few days later, in her office at the University, Annie was looking over notes for her next class when Frank Florescu abruptly walked in. She'd left her door open.

He had a small size Fed Ex box in his hand. Before saying anything, he closed her door. "Just got this from my aunt in Romania." He opened the box and showed her the contents—several small, white envelopes and two loose, handwritten notes. "It's the herbs for the gypsy cure I purchased from Celestina, and her directions on how to prepare them. My aunt gave her my check and offered to send them to me."

Her heart beating faster with trepidation, Annie took the two notes out of the box. She unfolded them. One was written on lined, yellowed, scratchpad paper, and the other on inexpensive flowered stationery. The handwritings didn't match and they weren't written in English.

"I can translate," Florescu said. He took the short letters from her and began reading the one on flowered stationery. "This is from my aunt. She says, 'Celestina put together these forest herbs for you. She didn't tell me what the herbs are. But she warned that the envelope with the dried pieces of a mushroom called the Death Cap is dangerous. Eating even half a mushroom would cause death. So do be careful when you use these herbs for your research, dear nephew.' And then she closes with regards from my relatives over there."

"A poisonous mushroom called Death Cap?" Annie said with trepidation. She looked up at Florescu as he stood beside her chair. "I don't think any of us should even touch it."

"I'll use latex medical gloves," Florescu said. "It must not have the same effect on a vampire. Maybe that's the most important part of the cure."

"Is Rafael supposed to eat it?" she asked with alarm.

"I'll read you Celestine's directions," he said with an impatient sigh and opened the note written on lined paper. "She says, 'Take a pinch of each herb, and a piece of the mushroom, and pulverize them. Mix them with a cup of blood, human or animal, and have the undead drink it. He must drink it at dawn just as the sun's rays are starting to appear on the horizon.'"

"Mix it with blood?" Annie said.

"Rafael must have some or know where to get it."

Annie thought of the blood bags in his refrigerator. She knew he drank from them, because they would quietly disappear, but he always consumed them when she wasn't there to see. Probably after she'd fallen asleep at night.

"Yes, he has blood. How would we pulverize the herbs and get it thoroughly mixed?"

"A blender?" Florescu suggested.

"Inez has one." Annie felt a bleak coldness come over her. "And what happens after he takes this concoction?"

He looked at the directions in his hand and shrugged. "Celestina doesn't say."

"Great," Annie said in a dour tone. "I don't think we should go through with this."

Florescu looked incensed. "Rafael wants to. And that was our deal. I supply him with the cure and he doesn't report me for trespassing. I'm keeping my end of the bargain, even purchased the remedy and paid for the shipping."

"You're only interested in your secret research," Annie said, hotly. "You don't care if Rafael lives or dies."

"Not as much as you. But I want to see if this remedy works. I could be the one who stamps out vampirism. You and Rafael would help in that cause. Isn't that a good thing?"

Annie inwardly rolled her eyes. Florescu and his delusions of grandeur. Even if he was hoping to accomplish something good, she didn't like Rafael to be his first test case.

"Well, isn't it?" he repeated.

"Yes. But we need to show all this to Rafael and see if he's still willing to go through with it."

"And you're hoping he'll change his mind," Florescu said in an accusatory tone.

"I have a right to my opinions. Would you want someone you loved to take this kind of risk?"

"You women!" he said with disgust. "Always ruled by your emotions. This is a scientific endeavor."

Annie wanted to answer back, but then it occurred to her that perhaps he never had a great love in his life. "We'll bring this to Rafael," she quietly responded. "It's his decision. Meanwhile, will you call Celestina and ask what's supposed to happen to the vampire after he takes the cure?"

Florescu gave her a nod. "Agreed. Tell Rafael I'll bring him the remedy before sunrise Sunday morning."

"So soon?"

"It's Wednesday today. You have three whole days to adjust your frail female mind to what your vampire lover wants. If he wants to be mortal, and I can do that for him, why should you have anything to say about it?"

Keeping her patience, Annie pursed her lips. "You know, Frank, I think relocating to Romania is a great idea for you. The sooner the better."

*Chapter 11*

In bed together all Saturday night, Rafael did his best to comfort and reassure Annie. He tried to convince her that taking Florescu's Romanian gypsy cure was the best thing for both of them. As she had in the past, she merely nodded her head in resignation. He made love with her to distract her. But after their shared climax of bliss, her face crumpled into tears and she cried on his chest.

"What if this is our last time?" she said in a broken voice.

For a moment Rafael could not reply. He had the same fear. "I still say, it's for the best," he told her, stroking her beautiful long hair. "I need to be mortal or we can never have a truly happy life. No more dark secrets to hide. I won't stay the same while you grow old. We'll age together. Isn't that what Florescu told you after he talked to Celestina again?"

"She told him the two vampires she says she cured are aging normally now. Claims she's kept in touch with them." Annie lifted her head to look at him. "But Frank finally admitted that there was a third vampire who wasn't cured. Celestina wasn't there to observe what happened, so she doesn't know why it failed. Frank insists her directions must not have been followed correctly. He made light of it, so I've tried to put it out of my mind, knowing one failure out of three probably wouldn't deter you."

"What happened to the vampire when the cure didn't work?" Rafael asked.

"Frank said he didn't know. Which makes me wonder if he's hiding the truth, that maybe the vampire perished." Annie swallowed, blinking back angry tears. "How do we really know if Frank or this Celestina are on the level? You decided to trust Frank after reading his thoughts, but I've never trusted him. And why should we rely on an aged herbalist we never met?"

"Apparently she's quite a religious woman. Remember Florescu said she was willing to swear on the Bible and by her beloved icons that she was telling him the truth?"

"I remember. But still . . . ," Annie murmured doubtfully. "Her remedy doesn't have a perfect track record."

Rafael sat up against his pillow and drew Annie against him, into his arms. "She sounds as religious as Inez. If you heard Inez swear that something was the truth, you'd believe her, wouldn't you?"

"Of course. But I know Inez. She's my friend. And Celestina won't be here to watch and make sure the cure is properly administered."

"Florescu has her written directions. He has a Ph.D. so he must be competent to follow them."

"So, you still want to go through with it," Annie said, sounding defeated and resigned. "I knew nothing I said would change your mind."

"It's for my love of you that I must go through with it." Rafael looked at the clock on the bed stand and felt an unexpected wave of anxiety rush through him. "It's four-thirty already. Florescu told you he'd be here by five, didn't he?"

Annie pushed away from him to read the clock. "Oh, my God, he'll be here soon. He was so eager the last time I talked to him, he'll probably get here early."

"We'd better get dressed."

Annie reluctantly nodded.

"Kiss me once more," he said, pulling her close. They kissed with deep, fervent emotion. He gently drew back and said, "I want to marry you, Annie. When I'm mortal again."

"I love you." She appeared to be fighting back new tears. "You'll always be my greatest love, my soul mate, whatever happens."

He pressed his forehead against hers for a long, silent, meaningful moment. Then summoning up courage—enough for both of them, he hoped—he took hold of her upper arms and looked in her eyes. "Let's get dressed."

Florescu knocked at Rafael's front door about ten minutes later. Wearing jeans and one of his white shirts, Rafael let him in.

The thin professor looked excited, breathing fast, eyes bright. He held up a box. "I brought it. You ready? Sunrise is in forty-five minutes."

"I'm ready," Rafael said, letting him in. As he was about to shut the door, he saw Inez and Francisco on their way over. Inez was carrying a blender from her kitchen.

"We'd like to be here with you, if that's okay," Francisco said.

"You're sure?" Rafael replied, feeling uneasy at having an audience for his transformation.

"We've known you for so long," Inez said, her face grave. "We don't want you to go through this alone."

Rafael tentatively gave them a nod and let them in. He would have preferred privacy, but he didn't want to hurt their feelings.

Annie came in and greeted all the visitors in a subdued manner, without her usual smile.

Florescu turned to Inez. "Good, you brought a blender."

"Annie said you would need one," Inez replied, handing it to him.

"And a blood bag," the professor said to Rafael.

Rafael rubbed his forehead, annoyed that his beloved friends would have to see the means by which he had physically thrived all these years. "I'll get one." He strode out of the room to his kitchen, opened the refrigerator and took out a bag. He held it in his hands for a moment, even now feeling the craving for the red liquid rising up inside him. He hoped God would see fit to allow him to survive this cure and liberate him from the humiliating need for blood.

Walking back to the living room, he handed the bag to Florescu. The professor seemed repulsed for a brief instant, but he took it. "Where can I plug in the blender?"

"Where the lamp is plugged in." Rafael pointed to the wall socket where the shaded lamp next to the leather sofa was connected.

Florescu bent down near the wall to plug in the appliance. "Now, as Celestina instructed, we pulverize a pinch of each of these dried herbs."

"And the Death Cap," Annie added in a grim tone.

Rafael lowered his gaze. Annie had told him about the deadly mushroom. He'd decided that since he was already dead, the mushroom couldn't harm him. Perhaps it was just the thing needed to bring his body back to life. Mortal life, not his undead existence.

Florescu set the blender on the sofa side table, beneath the lamp. He took purple medical gloves out of his pants pocket and pulled them on. Then he opened the box, began pulling out envelopes one by one, using his thumb and forefinger to take a bit of each to add to the blender. Lastly he broke off a yellowish-gray piece of the Death Cap and dropped it in. Everyone solemnly watched as he placed the cover on the blender and turned it on high speed. Soon the dry herbs and leaves, and the mushroom were pulverized into thick dust.

He'd set the blood bag on the sofa and picked it up now, examining its various connecting tubes. "How do you open one of these?" he asked.

With a sigh, Rafael stepped up. "Here." He took the bag out of Florescu's hands. Lifting it to his mouth, he used his sharp incisors, as he always did, to break into it. He carefully handed it back to the professor as a few drops of blood began to ooze out of the bag.

The blender had measurement markings and Florescu squeezed out one cup of blood, a look of distaste on his face as he did so. Rafael glanced at Annie, who silently observed with a barely repressed look of grim horror. Inez and Francisco appeared equally shaken.

Florescu gave the blood bag to Rafael, who took it back to the kitchen to throw away. When he returned, he saw the red concoction swirling vigorously in the blender on high speed. The professor turned off the appliance and inspected the blood mixed with specks of dark vegetal matter. "Looks good. Now we wait for dawn." He glanced at Rafael. "You're to drink it at the first rays of the sunrise."

"And what's supposed to happen exactly?" Inez asked as Annie turned away.

"Annie wanted me to call the herbalist again and ask her that," Florescu replied. "Celestina said that the herbs the vampire consumes will counteract the rays of the sun that ordinarily would turn him to ashes. It's a moment of transition from death back to life. He may feel like he's burning up. He may collapse. But he'll come to as a mortal." He raised his eyebrows, his gaze brightening. "She said the whole process only takes a few minutes. And she felt sure it would work because he's under a gypsy curse, and this is a gypsy remedy."

"Oh, yes, it all makes perfect sense." Annie's tone was full of sarcasm. She turned to Rafael. "Her remedy only worked in two out of three cases. One failed. That vampire may have perished! I don't think you should drink it."

Rafael clenched his jaw. He'd thought he'd convinced her this was the right thing to do.

Then Inez spoke up. "Don't, Rafael. We love you as you are."

Francisco placed his hand on Inez's shoulder. "I don't like it either, but it's Rafael's decision. We have to respect that."

"Absolutely," Florescu argued. "I've gone to great lengths to supply this cure for him. If he wants to go through with it, no one has the right to stop him."

"Shut up, Frank!" Annie said, her voice rough with anger. "All you care about is this experiment."

Rafael realized he had to speak sharply. "Enough. It is indeed my decision." He glanced at the clock on the fireplace mantle. "Dawn will come soon. Annie and Inez, I want you to go into the kitchen and wait there."

"What?" Annie said with alarm. "I will not! I want to be with you."

"I don't want you to watch," Rafael said sternly. "You're too emotional. You might interfere." In a more tender voice, he said, "Go, please. You, too, Inez." He looked at Francisco. "You can go with them, or stay here, whichever you choose."

"I'll stay," Francisco replied. He pointed to Florescu. "Keep an eye on him."

"Alright," Rafael said. He took a shocked Annie by the shoulders, turned her toward the kitchen and gave her a gentle push. "Please, Annie. I love you, but I don't want you to watch. Inez, you, too."

Inez began to head toward the kitchen.

"No!" Annie stubbornly stood her ground.

"There's no time to argue, Annie. I'm begging you, please go. It'll be less stressful for me if I don't have to worry about what you might see."

With a sigh Annie reluctantly followed Inez, but she turned to give Rafael a hurt look. "If it makes it easier for you, I'll go. But I should be with you."

Rafael nodded that he understood, but he waved her on to the kitchen. He blinked back tears, knowing he'd be stronger without her there. If he perished, he didn't want her to see his last moments as his body burned to ashes. He didn't want her to live with that horrible memory for the rest of her life.

When the two women had gone through the dining room and disappeared into the kitchen, he turned to Francisco. Extending his hand, he said, "You've been a loyal friend all these years. Most of those years, my only friend. It's more than I deserved."

Francisco's brown eyes glistened with sincerity as he shook hands. "Everything is okay between us. Know that."

"If things go wrong," Rafael told him, "I've written a will. It's in the top drawer of my office desk. Annie, you, and Inez are all included."

Francisco seemed surprised, speechless for a moment. "I pray nothing goes wrong."

Rafael smiled and patted Francisco's shoulder. He turned to Florescu. "I'm ready."

Florescu seemed keyed up with nervous energy. "Only a little while now," he said, looking at his watch. "Sunrise is at 5:24 this morning. I need to get my recording equipment ready."

"What recording equipment?" Rafael asked.

Florescu held up a shiny new tablet with a large screen. "This records both picture and sound. For my research."

"You're not going to record anything," Rafael said in a severe voice.

"But—"

"Give me that," Rafael said, pointing to the tablet.

"No!"

"Give it to me, or I'll rip it out of your hands and crack it over your head!" Rafael replied. "I still have my vampire strength."

Florescu looked shaken, but continued to argue. "I won't reveal your identity."

"You'd better not, and you are not to record this. I'd only appear in your film after I'm mortal. We vampires don't show up in photographs, remember?"

Florescu looked confused for a moment, during which Rafael snatched the tablet out of his hands and gave it to Francisco, who took it into Rafael's office.

"Sunrise is in a few minutes," Rafael said. "Let's get on with the cure."

"Okay," Florescu replied, sounding disappointed and annoyed. "I'll just write notes then." He went to the window next to the front door and opened the drapes. "Come over here," he told Rafael.

His chest constricting with trepidation, Rafael complied and stood by the window. Outside everything was still dark. Florescu went to the blender, removed the glass container and took off the top. He handed it to Rafael.

"No matter what happens," Rafael said, looking at the dark red liquid inside, "this is the last time I'll have to drink blood." It was a comforting thought.

Florescu checked his watch. "It's 5:24." Anxiously he looked out the window. "Should see some light any moment. Yes. There's a reddish cast forming along the horizon."

Rafael already could sense the rays beginning to assault his body and he instinctively grew fearful. Suddenly he felt horribly vulnerable and wanted to flee to his coffin. But his coffin was too far away for him to reach it in time. If he changed to wolf form, his thick coat of fur would protect him—

"Drink it!" Florescu ordered, pushing the container in Rafael's hand toward his mouth.

Fighting his urge to save himself by transmogrifying, Rafael gulped down the mixture of blood and herbs. The herbs gave it a revolting taste, making him gag. When he finished, Florescu took the empty container away and handed it to Francisco.

"How do you feel?" Florescu asked, studying him closely.

"The same." Rafael looked with fascination at the red sky of dawn. "Beautiful, isn't it?" He swayed on his feet and his hand went to his head.

"What's happening?" Florescu wanted to know.

"I'm feeling heavy, as if pulled toward the earth, and lightheaded at the same time. Warm now. No, hot! A speck of flesh against a fiery furnace." Weak from the intensity, he fell to his knees.

Francisco quickly went to him and tried to help him. But it was no use.

"I'm burning up!" Rafael cried as he saw smoke rising from his fingertips.

"Oh, God, no!" Francisco exclaimed.

"No, you can't be," Florescu argued. "Hold on."

Rafael began to shake uncontrollably as dizziness came over him. A reeling, tortuous feeling of internal flames overtook the core of his body. He had no strength left and as he fell forward, his arms could not keep him from hitting the floor.

"No use," he told Florescu in a final whisper that took the last of his strength. "You've failed."

He barely heard Florescu and Francisco shouting his name. Suddenly everything went black.

# # #

In the kitchen, Annie leaned against the counter, stifling sobs and trying to keep herself from hysteria. Inez clung to her, both to support her and to prevent her from running to Rafael.

"Don't go in there," Inez told her. "If you interrupt, it might disturb Rafael's delicate balance between death and life."

Annie grimaced, but nodded that she understood. Inez softly began to repeat a prayer, her rosary in hand.

Suddenly they both looked up at the sound of voices calling Rafael's name. They hurried to the living room.

Annie screamed in shock when she saw Rafael's inert body on the floor, his complexion gray. "He didn't survive?"

"He collapsed," Francisco said, looking up as he hovered over Rafael. "He said he was burning up. Smoke was coming from his hands." He felt Rafael's wrist. "I can't find a pulse. He's gone!"

Annie and Inez held on to each other weeping. Annie felt totally bereft, weak with grief.

"But he's *not* gone," Florescu argued. "The sun hasn't turned him to ashes."

He shoved Francisco out of the way, then turned Rafael's body to lay face up. The front of Rafael's shirt looked damp and a thin vapor rose up from his chest.

"Anybody have a mirror?" Florescu asked.

Annie stopped breathing in the middle of a sob. "Why?"

"Just get one," the professor ordered.

Too muddled by overwhelming sorrow to argue, Annie thought of the small, round mirror she kept in her purse. She went to the bedroom, got it and returned. As she gave it to Florescu, she'd begun to wonder if he thought there was still hope.

Florescu held the mirror over Rafael in such a way that he could tilt the glass and look in it. "His reflection shows up." He set the mirror on the floor and pushed up Rafael's lip, exposing some of his teeth. "His incisors are normal. He's no longer a vampire."

"Then he died at peace," Inez said quietly as she took up her rosary again.

Florescu felt the side of Rafael's neck. "I think there's a faint pulse."

"Is he breathing?" Annie asked. She picked up the mirror and held it beneath Rafael's nose. A faint dew of condensation appeared.

"Who knows CPR?" Annie asked.

Francisco moved closer. "I learned it a long time ago."

"Press on his chest, and I'll breathe into his mouth," Annie said.

She and Francisco worked to resuscitate Rafael. Though not brought up in any religion, Annie found herself silently praying that their efforts would bring Rafael to life.

"His complexion has more color in it," Florescu said, looking on. "Don't you think?"

Francisco and Annie drew back to study Rafael's face. All at once, with a sudden gasp, Rafael began to breathe on his own.

Annie tapped her fingers against his cheek. "Rafael, can you hear me?"

He opened his eyes and looked into her face. His brown eyes shone with adoration. "Annie," he whispered.

"It worked!" Florescu exclaimed, jubilant. "I've cured a vampire!"

"Can you sit up?" Francisco asked, supporting Rafael, hands beneath his shoulders.

"Is he really alright?" Inez asked, stepping closer.

Rafael tried to speak. "My mouth . . .so dry."

"I'll get water," Inez said and hurried off.

"I'm alive?" Rafael asked Annie.

"You seem to be. Look in this mirror." She picked it up and held it in front of him.

He peered into it. His eyes widened. "That's me?"

"Yes," she said, laughing. "And your incisors aren't sharp anymore."

As he pressed his finger against one of his teeth, Inez returned with a glass of water. She gave it to Annie, who held the glass as he took a sip. Then, like a man who had come across a desert, he took the glass from her with both hands and gulped the water down.

"The sun's rays must have dehydrated him," Florescu said, observing Rafael closely. "That was vapor coming from his fingers, not smoke. How do you feel?"

Rafael set the glass on the floor and blinked. "Thirsty. Disoriented. Weak." His eyes widened. "My vampire strength is gone. It's gone. I'm ordinary." He shook his head. "I didn't think I'd miss it."

"You mean, you do?" Annie asked. "You wanted to be an ordinary mortal."

He looked in her eyes. "I did, didn't I?"

"And now you're disappointed?"

His gaze took on a steady glow. "No." He smiled. "I'm just like you now. You're so beautiful in daylight. I had no idea. We can live a normal life together."

"Yeah, that's great," Florescu interrupted with impatience. "How do you feel sitting in the sun from the window? Any ill effect?"

Rafael turned and squinted at the soft morning light streaming in. "It's bright. I'm not used to it. But I want to go outside. See the earth in daylight."

Francisco helped him up from the floor and steadied him as he wobbled on his feet.

Rafael stood still for a moment and took a long breath. "I'm okay."

"We'll go out with you," Annie said, taking his hand.

Annie and Rafael walked out the front door onto the gravel driveway. Francisco stayed close by his side. Annie turned to see Florescu eagerly following them out, as did Inez.

Rafael stopped and slowly turned, keeping hold of Annie's hand so that she took the slow turn with him. She could see his excitement as they observed the hilly horizon beneath the blue sky, the desert chaparral, the duplex and stables, the corral and his Spanish tiled stucco ranch house. Annie felt as if she were seeing it all anew along with him.

She noticed tears streaming down his face, his eyes wide and shining with joy.

"Isn't it incredible?" he exclaimed. "All the colors! The azure sky. How white the clouds are. The terracotta roof. Look, the cactus has yellow flowers!" He pointed to a patch of prickly pear cactus growing near the front door. He gazed at Annie again. "And your cheeks, fragile pink."

Annie hugged him, too choked with happy tears to speak.

Rafael looked at Inez and Francisco, and at Florescu. "I'm grateful to you all for making this possible."

# # #

At rest, lying face up in her big RV parked on a side street in Cottonwood, Maisie suddenly opened her eyes, feeling strange. All at once she took in a huge gasp of air. This was odd. It had never happened before when she slept in her coffin during daylight hours. She continued feeling the need to breathe deeply and noticed that her usual profound lethargy was gone. She felt life in her limbs and was able to lift her head. Something was wrong. Was it sunset already? It seemed way too soon.

Maisie raised her hands to the lid of her wood coffin and pushed it up just a crack. Shallow beams of light crept in. She could tell it was sunlight, not lamplight. Why didn't she feel the rays attacking her body? She pushed the lid open further. Still no ill effect. She opened it entirely and sat up, feeling a little dizzy. When the dizziness passed, she climbed out of the coffin and hesitantly went to a window near the table in the RV's compact kitchen, which she never used. The blinds on the window were closed, but sunlight was leaking through. How could that be? She pulled on the cord to open them just slightly, and more light poured in. She squinted, unused to the brightness accosting her eyes, and pulled them shut again.

What was going on? Her hand flew to her mouth in shock. *Am I mortal again?*

It occurred to her that she could tell for sure if she looked in a mirror. She hurried to the vehicle's small, unused bathroom, where a built-in mirror she'd never bothered to remove hung over the wash basin. When she got in front of the glass she was shocked to see her reflection.

"Oh, no! No, no!" she exclaimed. "Why? Why??" She opened her mouth exposing her incisors. They were small and rounded. "No!" she exclaimed in anguish. "Why am I not a vampire anymore?"

Furious, she made a fist and slammed her hand against the mirror to smash the image of herself into smithereens. But the glass didn't break and her hand hurt. A new sense of angry horror claimed her as she realized she'd lost her superhuman strength. She looked at her hand and saw a red bruise forming along the side of her fist.

"I'm a puny mortal again," she lamented, rubbing her hand to ease the pain.

She paused to collect her wits, then thought of Rafael. He could turn her again.

Unless the same thing had happened to him . . . ?

Frantic, she rushed out of the tiny bathroom to the front of the RV, squinting in the sharp sunlight from the windows. She slid behind the driver's seat and turned on the ignition.

*Chapter 12*

Rafael kept his patience, cheerfully content to be alive and sitting in his living room with Annie in the daylight, as Florescu pumped him with questions and took copious notes on a large pad of lined paper. Francisco had left to look after the Appaloosas. Inez had departed with him.

All at once he heard a vehicle on the gravel driveway, and then a sharp knock at his front door. Florescu looked annoyed at the disruption, but Rafael got up from the couch to open the door.

"Maisie," Rafael exclaimed, shocked to see her furious blue eyes and honey blond hair radiant with color in the sunshine. "You're cured?"

"Cured!" Maisie couldn't seem to contain her ferocity. "You've reverted, too? What happened? Why are we feeble mortals again?"

Florescu came to the door. He gawked at Maisie in astonishment. "You were a vampire?"

"Who's he?" Maisie asked Rafael with indignation.

"Dr. Frank Florescu," Rafael told her. "He made me mortal again with a remedy from Romania."

Maisie stared at Rafael in disbelief. "You mean, you *asked* him to?"

Rafael thought over how it had all come about. "Yes, in a manner of speaking, I did. He's something of an expert on vampires." He turned to Florescu.

"Thank you for saying so," Florescu replied with a polite nod. He shifted his gaze to Maisie again, his eyes alive with curiosity. "When exactly did you regain your mortality?"

"A little while ago. Do you know how to change me back?"

Rafael furrowed his brow in dismay. He noticed the professor seemed a bit flummoxed.

"No," Florescu replied. "You're so very beautiful. Why would you want to return to such an unholy state?"

"Unholy?" Maisie repeated. "It's the best existence ever! I had superhuman strength. Stayed young and had fabulous sex. Why would I want to be an ordinary woman again?" Her eyes narrowed. "If you're the one who caused this, I'll claw your eyes out!" She raised her hand, long pink-lacquered fingernails projecting. But then she looked at her hand, eyes squinting with pain. "You see this bruise? I can't even smash glass anymore."

The professor, who had back away, swallowed. "How did you become a vampire?"

"Rafael turned me decades ago," she replied. "We were lovers. I begged him to."

"And then she ran off," Rafael quietly added.

Florescu seemed preoccupied in thought. "I'm beginning to understand what must have happened," the professor murmured as his eyes brightened. "Rafael was turned into a vampire by a gypsy's curse. He sired you," he said, pointing to Maisie. "When Rafael took the gypsy cure, the curse was broken. And that apparently had a ripple effect on you, Maisie. You've been freed from the curse as well. Amazing," Florescu said. "I've got to get this down in my notes."

As the professor went to get his pen and paper, Maisie's eyes followed him with resentment. "What if I don't want to be freed? Huh?" she called after him. "If you're such a big expert, you ought to figure out some way to turn me back!"

# # #

Quietly standing just behind Rafael, Annie looked on with satisfaction. When she'd seen that it was Maisie at the door, she'd hurried to be near him, unsure what the seductive blonde might want. She'd been stunned—and relieved—to learn that Maisie was no longer a vampire. While they were talking, Annie thought of Brent and wondered if this meant he would no longer be under Maisie's power.

All at once Annie heard her cell phone ringing. She'd left it on the dining room table and hurried there to find the call was from Brent.

"Annie? Something odd has happened." Brent's voice was just above a whisper. "Zoe's home. I don't want her to overhear. The marks are gone. You know what I'm talking about. Wondered if you know why?"

"I think I do," she told Brent. "Better come over here right now. Everything will be explained. Leave Zoe at home."

After ending the call, she walked back into the living room. Florescu, trying to take charge as usual, was telling Maisie, "Take a seat. I need to ask you more questions."

"I don't take orders from you," Maisie shot back, keeping her place in the doorway.

To Annie's amusement, Florescu appeared stymied. He looked down on women, but a stunning blonde could obviously get the better of him. Who knew?

"Maisie," Rafael said, "if you cooperate, it might be that the professor can eventually come up with a solution for you."

Maisie seemed to rethink her stubborn stance and reluctantly walked into the living room. As she took a seat on one of the easy chairs, Annie walked up to Rafael.

"Brent just phoned," she whispered in his ear. "The marks on his neck have disappeared. I told him to come over."

Rafael smiled. "Excellent." He gave Annie a hug. "Everything's coming around right."

They sat together on the couch again as Florescu cross-examined an impatient Maisie.

Annie observed the exquisite ex-vampiress with a mixture of feelings. Relief for Brent's sake, and some trepidation. Maisie still appeared so young and beautiful, Annie knew men couldn't help but find her irresistible.

Annie glanced at Rafael and was surprised to meet his eyes as he appeared to be studying her.

He took Annie's hand. "For me, you are the only woman in the world. No one else exists," he whispered.

Annie smiled and squeezed his hand, embarrassed that he'd intuited her thoughts, but grateful for his affirmation.

Soon Brent arrived in record time. When Annie heard his knock, she let him in.

"What's going on?" he asked as he looked at the people gathered in the living room. "Maisie! Rafael. It's daytime . . . ."

Rafael rose to greet him. "We're cured. Sit by Annie. I'll grab a chair from my office."

"What?" Brent's eyes questioned Annie as he sat down on the couch.

"It's true." Annie introduced Frank Florescu and told Brent everything.

"The cure worked," Rafael said, bringing a chair into the room. "And because I turned Maisie, the cure extended to her. I'm beyond happy. She's not."

"Better believe I'm not!" Maisie muttered.

Florescu, looking startled, asked Brent, "You knew their secret?"

"Maisie's my girlfriend," Brent explained. He pressed his fingertips to the side of his neck. "She . . . um . . ."

"Bit you?" Florescu said.

"She did. But this morning when I was shaving I saw the marks were completely healed. And she drank from me only last night."

Florescu scribbled hurriedly on his pad of paper. "Incredible. This is fabulous information."

Brent looked at Maisie. "Are you okay?"

"I'm not an immortal anymore," she retorted. "What do you think?"

Annie saw that Brent seemed taken aback and felt bad for him. "Your life will be normal again," she told him. "Zoe will never have to know."

Brent seemed to take in what she was saying. He looked relieved. "Thank God for that." He turned his eyes to Maisie again. "What about us?"

Maisie's eyes softened a bit, but nevertheless she replied, "It's all changed, Brent. I won't be your stupid little girlfriend. I really like Zoe, but she was in the way. Once she was off to college, I figured I'd be free to turn you. Then we could have been vampires together. The sex would have been unimaginable. But that possibility is all gone."

"I thought you loved me," Brent said.

A trace of guilt shadowed Maisie's blue eyes. "I did. Sort of. You look so much like Gable, it was fun to explore that fantasy when you were under my power. But you're not anymore. If I stayed with you, you'd start asserting yourself and telling me what to do, how to behave. Zoe told me how you treated her mother. And why Annie decided not marry you. I won't behave for you or anyone."

"Maisie thinks only of herself," Rafael told Brent. "I learned that the hard way."

Brent appeared crestfallen. "So, what will you do?" he asked Maisie. "Leave me?"

Maisie bowed her head for a moment, then looked up again. "Guess so. Unless the professor here knows some way to change me back."

"You'd only stay with me if you're a vampire?" Brent said. "You never really loved me." Sadly he shook his head. "Well then, thank God you're cured. I'm glad I don't feel you intruding my mind anymore. You made me obsessed with you. You're a beautiful girl, but I'll be happy not to have you in my life. Or in Zoe's either."

Maisie blithely nodded. "Well, that's settled. Fun while it lasted. Say goodbye to Zoe for me."

Brent leaned back into the couch looking dumbfounded. Annie had to feel sorry for Brent, being so rudely rejected by Maisie under such strange circumstances.

Everyone was quiet for a moment, apparently at a loss what to say.

Florescu broke the silence. "I need to ask more questions."

The professor pressed Brent about how he'd felt being under a vampire's power. He finished up asking Maisie and Rafael what it was like to lose their superhuman abilities. They had different perspectives.

"The only thing I might miss is shapeshifting to wolf form. I did enjoy that," Rafael said. "But it's easy to give that up for a happy life with Annie."

"You were capable of transmogrification?" Florescu said, astonished all over again.

"How come I never got to change into a wolf?" Maisie demanded to know.

"I was turned by a wolf-like manifestation when the gypsy curse took effect," Rafael said. "Seemed like a real wolf that attacked me, but it must have been supernatural. Did you ever *try* to change to wolf form?" he asked Maisie.

"I never knew it was possible," Maisie shot back. "You never told me you could do that."

"You didn't stick around long enough for me to confide in you," Rafael said dryly.

Annie quietly smiled at the prickly animosity between the two former vampires. Rafael glanced at her, caught her expression and chuckled. But the humor was lost on Florescu, who was feverishly writing new notes, while Brent remained subdued.

Eventually Brent got up from the sofa. "I think I'll leave now. Things to do at the ranch."

Florescu objected, but Brent ignored him. Annie walked with him to the door.

"I can see you're upset," Annie said as she stepped outside with him. "But it's really all for the best. Sounds like Maisie had plans to turn you once Zoe went to college."

Brent looked up at the sky. "It's unimaginable. Maisie really took over my life. Hope she leaves town for good."

"Me, too," Annie agreed. After a pause, she asked, "Do you mind if I keep in touch with Zoe? Can she come to visit? I'm very fond of her."

Brent nodded. "Sure, she can visit. And I'm glad you and I are on friendly terms. I can see you and Rafael were meant to be. Maybe someday I'll find the right girl for me."

"I hope so," Annie said. "You're handsome and successful. Find a woman you can admire as your equal. I wish you well."

He thanked her and went to his pick-up.

Anne walked back inside to find Maisie, temper aroused again, peppering Frank Florescu with questions.

"What kind of expert are you?" she asked in a challenging tone. "You want answers from us, but you give none in return. If I still had fangs I'd bite you! Focus on my question: How can I get back to being a vampire?"

The professor looked like he felt pressured, a little scared, and was growing agitated. "I told you, I don't know."

"You knew about the cure for the gypsy curse. Do you know a gypsy who can put the same curse on me?"

"Are you crazy?" Florescu asked. "Who wants to be under a curse?"

"Me!"

"I . . . I'd have to ask my contact in Romania if she still knows any gypsies. The cure is very old, a recipe she got when she was young from an aged gypsy woman. Everything's gotten modern. No one goes around asking gypsies for curses anymore." But then his expression changed. "Unless . . . ."

"What?" Maisie prompted.

"Vampires still inhabit some rural areas in Romania. You could go and try to find one."

"To turn me," Maisie said excitedly. "Do you know what places I should go to?"

Florescu reluctantly nodded. "Yes. But please listen—these are unevolved vampires. Not like Rafael. They aren't civilized. They won't be gentle with you."

"I'll take my chances," Maisie said. "Will you go to Romania with me? You can hide and observe when I find a vampire to turn me."

He appeared to grow pale. "That would be dangerous. I wouldn't want to be anywhere near an active vampire."

"Oh, pooh. Well, then, take me to the right place during the day and leave me there."

Florescu hesitated.

"Come on, Dr. Frank," she said, turning on her sweetest smile. "You caused me to be mortal against my will, so you owe me. We'll have fun traveling together to Romania. I promise," she said, leaning forward just so, making her cleavage show, "you won't regret it."

Florescu's eyes took on a carnal glint as he stared at her generous bosom. "Um . . . well, I am planning to move to Romania. I can take you with me when I go."

"Cool," she said, looking genuinely happy now. "When?"

"I'm not sure yet," he said, befuddled.

"We'll help you pack," Annie offered, amazed to see Frank so easily besotted and seduced.

"Sounds like a good solution," Rafael chimed in. "You can continue your vampire studies in Romania, as you've planned, with the help of a former and soon-to-be-again vampire. Make her promise to visit you after she's found a vampire to turn her, and she can be your secret source of information." He glanced at Maisie. "You'd have an important role to play in educating the public about vampires."

"Even more cool," Maisie purred. She wet her lips in a tantalizing way. "Frankie, why don't we go to your house now and start making plans?"

Florescu nodded eagerly as a bead of sweat ran down his face. "Sure."

Maisie and Florescu left with barely a word of goodbye to Annie and Rafael. Which didn't bother Annie in the least. She was glad to see them go.

Alone for the first time since he'd become mortal, she and Rafael embraced.

"I'm the most contented man on the planet," Rafael said, stroking her hair back from her face. "You and I can finally be happy."

"Finally," she repeated with a smile. "No more darkness. Only sunshine and love."

*Epilogue*

Inez and Francisco were married in the church they both attended, with Rafael and Annie, Brent and Zoe, and all the ranch hands and the church's congregation in attendance. They lived happily together in the duplex, having removed the door adjoining their two apartments. Francisco continued training Rafael's Appaloosas. Pearl Girl won blue ribbons and several lucrative offers were made by interested buyers, but Inez would not part with her.

After Rafael obtained forged identification documents, he and Annie were married by a judge in a quiet civil ceremony, with Inez and Francisco there to witness the wedding. Annie gave up her condo and lived joyfully with Rafael at Rancho de la Noche. She continued teaching, though she decided to take off a semester when she became pregnant. She gave birth to a healthy baby, a boy, whom they named Joaquin.

Maisie accompanied Frank Florescu to Romania. Annie and Rafael did not hear from them again.

## About the Author

Lori Herter grew up in the suburbs of Chicago, graduated from the University of Illinois, Chicago Campus, and worked for several years at the Chicago Association of Commerce & Industry. She married her husband, Jerry, a CPA and they moved to Southern California a few decades ago. They still live there with their cat, Jasmine. They have traveled extensively in the U.S., Canada, Europe, New Zealand, Australia, and Tahiti. Lori's favorite destination of all is Ireland.

Lori has written romance novels published by Dell Candlelight Romances, Silhouette, and Harlequin. Some of these books are currently available as ebooks on Amazon and Barnes & Noble. She also wrote a four-book romantic vampire series published by Berkley with the titles OBSESSION, POSSESSION, CONFESSION, and ETERNITY. Her most recent work published by Berkley is her novella, "Cimarron Spirit" in the New York Times bestseller, EDGE OF DARKNESS. "Cimarron Secrets" is the sequel to "Cimarron Spirit" and "Cimarron Seductress" is the third novella in the Cimarron Series.

Lori's website is: www.loriherter.com

Printed in Great Britain
by Amazon